THE UNEXPECTED ELEMENTS of LOVE

KATE LEGGE is a multi-award-winning journalist who has covered politics and social affairs in Canberra, Sydney, Melbourne and Washington. She now writes for the *Australian* and lives in Melbourne with her husband and their two children. This is her first novel.

THE UNEXPECTED ELEMENTS of LOVE

KATE LEGGE

VIKING
an imprint of
PENGUIN BOOKS

VIKING

Published by the Penguin Group
Penguin Group (Australia)
250 Camberwell Road, Camberwell, Victoria 3124, Australia
(a division of Pearson Australia Group Pty Ltd)
Penguin Group (USA) Inc.
375 Hudson Street, New York, New York 10014, USA
Penguin Group (Canada)
90 Eglinton Avenue East, Suite 700, Toronto ON M4P 2Y3, Canada
(a division of Pearson Penguin Canada Inc.)
Penguin Books Ltd
80 Strand, London WC2R 0RL, England
Penguin Ireland
25 St Stephen's Green, Dublin 2, Ireland
(a division of Penguin Books Ltd)
Penguin Books India Pvt Ltd
11 Community Centre, Panchsheel Park, New Delhi – 110 017, India
Penguin Group (NZ)
Cnr Airborne and Rosedale Roads, Albany, Auckland, New Zealand
(a division of Pearson New Zealand Ltd)
Penguin Books (South Africa) (Pty) Ltd
24 Sturdee Avenue, Rosebank, Johannesburg 2196, South Africa

Penguin Books Ltd, Registered Offices: 80 Strand, London WC2R 0RL, England
First published by Penguin Books Australia Ltd, 2006
10 9 8 7 6 5 4 3 2 1

Text copyright © Kate Legge 2006
The moral right of the author has been asserted

All rights reserved. Without limiting the rights under copyright reserved above, no part of this publication may be reproduced, stored in or introduced into a retrieval system, or transmitted, in any form or by any means (electronic, mechanical, photocopying, recording or otherwise), without the prior written permission of both the copyright owner and the above publisher of this book.

Cover design by Marina Messiha © Penguin Group (Australia)
Text design by Susannah Low © Penguin Group (Australia)
Cover photograph by Martin Barraud/Getty
Typeset in Sabon by Post Pre-press Group, Brisbane, Queensland
Printed in Australia by McPherson's Printing Group, Maryborough, Victoria

National Library of Australia
Cataloguing-in-Publication data:

Legge, Kate, 1957- .
  Unexpected elements of love.

  ISBN-13: 978 0 670 07033 6.
  ISBN-10: 0 670 07033 5.

  I. Title.

A823.4

www.penguin.com.au

*To my mother, Alison,
who never grew old*

HARRY WAITS IN the car for his mother. He doesn't like visiting her office, because of the lift. When the doors slide shut his heart beats so fast he can't breathe. He always takes the stairs. Stairs can't malfunction.

Wind, thunder, lightning, cyclones, storms, injections, lifts, the dark, being left alone in the house, being left alone, mashed potato, being left alone. These are some of his unfavourite things.

He sinks down in the seat so that all he can see through a letterbox slot of window is the sky. He has a chart of clouds on his bedroom wall. 'Eye the sky and be weather wise' it says. There are sixteen pictures of white puffballs, some stretched thin like chewy, others bunched in mushroom shapes. 'Cumulonimbus calvus,' he recites slowly, for the low cauliflower cloud that means 'get under the bed quick'.

At the sound of his name being called, he wriggles up to look around. A woman on the other side of the street is yelling to a *little girl with a straw hat on her head.* 'Hurry,' *the mother calls urgently, for the second time, but the girl dawdles, entranced by an elderly man standing on the corner nearest Harry. The man is wearing a life jacket over his black shirt.*

Perhaps he's shipwrecked. Harry wonders how the old man's boat has come to grief.

The wind springs up and whips the little girl's hat off her head, spinning it like a saucer. She chases it out on to the road.

'No,' Harry screams, but the old man's voice is louder and the girl stops a second before a car crushes her hat under its wheels.

The old man locks eyes with Harry, relieved that what they both imagined has not come to pass. He smiles at the boy as if he understands how trouble haunts him. Then the man picks up the hat with its red ribbon flattened into the brim and turns it over in his rough hands. He slips it into a scruffy leather satchel slung over a shoulder. Harry stares after him, mystified, as the man saunters on his way.

THE CITY IS MELTING. Last night the house continued to bake long after the sun had gone from the sky. Janet dampened the children's bedsheets to cool their restless bodies. 'Mel, Harry,' she shouts now, herding them out the door, down the steps and into the car. Late as usual. The backs of her bare legs stick to the vinyl seat and a trickle of sweat collects in the cavity between her breasts.

She reverses out of the driveway too quickly but there's no crunch of toys or bicycle frame under the tyres, only a whine of complaint as duco grazes the bitumen. The bump tickles Harry. Their neighbour, Bernard, is hand-watering a weeping cherry and he aims the nozzle at the car window where Harry's impish face is pressed flat against the glass, mouth open, tongue out, bubbling excitedly. Harry slides open the window and leans his whippet-thin body halfway out to deliver a parting shout. 'I'll report you to the water police,' he laughs, and flops back in his seat as Janet speeds off.

Bernard has been fined once already this summer, when his automatic sprinkling system came on at 2 a.m., sending precious liquid trickling down the hill. He insists the system has a mind of its own but truth be known he has never read the operating manual and reprogramming is beyond him. Water restrictions seem out of place in this suburb that floats, snips of ocean blue bobbing into view around a corner, then gone again.

Janet switches from the FM breakfast show chosen by her daughter, Mel, to the public broadcaster, which is reporting news of torrential floods in India and Bangladesh – the death toll is rising with the tide. There was a photograph in this morning's paper of a young man waist deep in a muddy swirl, one arm raised to hold steady the television set perched on his turbaned head as he concentrated on safe passage. Janet is swept along on the radio's description of fluid mayhem, when she catches Harry's alarm in the rear-view mirror. His pipe-cleaner limbs are scrunched tight and he is chewing the collar of his shirt, wide eyed at what he hears. Mel has her nose in a book, oblivious to what is happening inside the car or on the subcontinent.

Janet flips the radio back to music and chat and rounds the corner faster than the fifty-kilometre speed limit, braking sharply behind a four-wheel drive come to rest at the tail end of a long line of traffic. Every year another apartment tower rears up as glimpses of harbour are subdivided and framed behind glass, attracting auction bids to rival the Picasso that Sotheby's sold last week for a record price. Hundreds of new high-rise units boast underground warrens that seem to breed cars overnight. The ten-minute trip to school now takes half an hour or more, even with a snatch of luck and green lights.

'Mr Picket always runs the yellow ones,' Harry urges her when she plays safe. That's because Mr Picket is fifty going on eighteen, she thinks. He has to keep up with a second wife much younger than his first bride, who is the mother of Harry's friend.

The line of cars crawls forward too slowly. 'What is going on here?' Janet snaps.

'It's just peak hour, Mum,' says her unflappable daughter, without lifting her gaze from her book. Her name is Melinda, but the full mouthful is saved for a passport application or the labouring of every syllable when she's in trouble, which is beyond rare. In her eleventh year now, Mel is a steady soul. Janet guesses that adolescence will hardly rock her.

'Is there an accident?' Harry croaks, poking his head up over the top of the seat.

'Harry! Seatbelt!' Janet orders.

He slumps back and clips himself in and props his feet against the front seat, jiggling restlessly. Mel turns the page and ignores him. They are unalike. She's fair and straight. He's dark and curly. She wakes in a bed tucked neat, as if no one has lain between the sheets; her conversation is as economical and sound as her sleep. He's into everything by day, then up and down all night in a game of musical beds that often ends in the small hours with their father, Nick, flaked out on Harry's bed, under his dreamcatcher.

'You'll miss your swimming heats,' Janet says to Harry. Fearing the worst is something she's inherited from her mother, along with the habit of clutching screwed-up tissues in her hand. 'Oh my God, goggles. Did you put them in your bag?'

Harry shrugs.

'Well, you'll have to borrow some.'

She breathes deeply and thinks of the lesson she learned as a student backpacker riding third-class on a crowded overnight train to Calcutta. All things pass. All journeys end. Of course, they must.

'Mum,' Harry says, derailing her thoughts. 'What's a monsoon?'

She's a weather presenter. She knows these answers off pat. But she has to be careful with Harry so that the facts don't swamp him. 'A monsoon is when the sky has a really good cry, but it doesn't happen here. Only in India.'

'How far away is India? How many hours?'

'It depends on who's driving,' she teases. 'If Mr Picket's in the pilot seat, you could be there in a blink.'

A smile dances across Harry's lips.

'Monsoons happen every year in the tropics. It gets hotter and hotter and hotter until everyone is dreaming of rain. The Indian weather bureau can tell almost to the day when the skies will burst.' As soon as these words slip out of her mouth, she wants them back.

He pounces. 'What do you mean, burst? How does the sky burst?' Only eight, and such a worrywart.

'It's just another way of describing rain.' She moves on quickly, hoping information overload will quieten the whirring of his imagination. 'Countries have different climates. The Indians expect heavy rains to fall because the wet season is part of their life, like Christmas. But it came early this year.' She's not about to dwell on the reason why, the warming.

'You know what I've told you,' she soothes. 'Climate is what you expect and weather is what you get.'

The cars ahead finally pick up speed and as she accelerates Janet can see what has caused the bottleneck. An aluminium walking frame mounts the kerb, an elderly woman hunched over its handles, dragging her feet.

Janet swallows her annoyance briskly. It's the tempo she brings to every chore, from plucking out the grey that speckles her straight black hair to the deft way she switches lanes to beat urban gridlock, her blinker marking life as precisely as a metronome.

AGE OR THE arthritis crippling her 74-year-old body is turning Beth Worboys from a stoic who once tilted at martyrdom into a feisty, bloody-minded senior. Once she would have muttered all the way to the zebra crossing at the bottom of the hill. Now she buggers the peak-hour traffic. Using her frame as a shield, she jaywalks from one side of the street to the other at whim, daring the delivery vans to run her down. She is deaf to the bleat of horns, just as she once ignored labourers' wolf whistles in the days when she rode a bike everywhere, her lean limbs winning lustful stares. She snubs the bleating 'don't walk' sign at traffic lights with the same cheerful contempt. So far she has refused to get one of those electric scooters that have liberated the walking wounded, relying instead on the wheelie walking frame she calls Cuz. It's her constant companion, part security blanket, part life support. Her dear friend Mora, who hasn't a creaking joint or loose cog, calls it the 'chrome bar stool'.

Arthritis first struck when Beth was forty. Bending down to pull a tray of hot pies from the school canteen oven, she suddenly felt as if her knees were on fire. The pain grows stronger with the years but she wears it determinedly, counting the paces from the front door to the car. Mora nags her to get a hip replacement but she resists, fearful of what would happen once it wore out. Her husband, Roy, had concurred, and Beth can't help wondering if he had been afraid of upsetting the fine balance of reciprocity underpinning their relationship.

His career as a sculptor has long shaped their life together. He has relied on her good-natured sacrifice and she has shared in his success. He fetches and carries to lighten her load; she steadies his emotional swings. But if in her dependency she were to lean too heavily upon him, perhaps his resentment would topple them both.

Beth has done everything she can to hinder the deterioration. She's tried to loosen up by swimming therapeutic laps in the outdoor pool beside the harbour where the choppy waves slap up against the concrete tub of chlorinated water. When the pool was built, Sydney's swimmers were thrilled to leave behind the harbour, with its dead gulls and animal carcasses. Now signs warn of invisible parasites lurking in the clear blue pool, which has been converted into an aquatic centre with lanes calibrated for fast and slow swimmers. The day she was almost mowed down by the North Sydney Tadpoles, Beth decided to stick with walking.

She has always loved to walk. You don't need crampons or goggles or personal trainers or anything special in the wardrobe department, just a pair of comfortable shoes. And you can venture deep inside wilderness, following the merest of tracks to a place where the pink trigger orchid embroiders the mossy carpet of old-growth forest. She first met Roy on a walk, a four-day trek along the Freycinet Peninsula. He joked that he came to know every dimple on her thighs, and not just because her legs outshone the scraggy limbs protruding from the shorts of the other bushwalkers. He said her shapely pins had lured him up the slopes of Mt Graham and kept his thoughts off his own aching calf muscles.

Years later Roy cast her legs crudely in bronze. Beth was furious and still averts her eyes whenever she visits the gallery courtyard where they tower majestically, like giant sequoias, giving visitors a crick in the neck if they do as the title suggests and 'Go On, Look Up Her Skirt'.

If only such a lure could draw her up this hill. The promise of meeting Dale, her daughter, lends encouragement, but the morning seems hotter than it should be with the sun still low. Pausing under the wisps of shade thrown by a tall lemon-scented gum, she swallows to moisten her mouth, which feels as parched as the balding nature strip. The leaves on the hibiscus over a garden fence hang limp, curling at the edges. An empty plastic bottle of spring water, flattened by cars, skitters into the gutter. She used to pick up loose rubbish but the task now defeats her.

Breathing the tang of gum, she watches the churning river of cars and sees a white stationwagon pull over on the crest of the hill. A young woman with spiky bleached hair gets out, then bends back into the car to kiss the driver. She limbers like a flamingo, her long legs splaying from a hip-hugging skirt. Beth admires them. She is allowed to stare because she is invisible to everybody, with the exception of children, who covet her portable climbing gym. The amorous farewell dams the flow of traffic and there is a honking blare of protest before the stationwagon sails off over the hill. Beth repositions her hands on Cuz's handlebars and departs base camp for the summit.

When they moved to Kirribilli forty years ago there was a milk bar, a grocery store and a butcher with a sawdust floor and heavy wooden cutting blocks. He always called her Mrs G, even though she was Mrs W, and she never had the heart to correct him. The new management boasts a marketing degree, and the beef, like the banter, doesn't come roughly hewn but neatly coiffed into gourmet cuts or seasoned with marinades. Roy does most of the cooking these days. He likes the chemistry of it, and it keeps Beth off her feet. Their meals have become increasingly haphazard affairs as he becomes immersed in what they suppose will be his last significant public commission, a sculpture to adorn the forecourt of the meteorological bureau in Canberra. He's told her that he finds posterity's hot breath on his neck unpleasant in a climate already warm. She doesn't like to bother him when he is working; he stays in his studio out the back until after the evening news, when darkness falls and the night air cools.

She turns the corner into the suburb's main street and there is a quickening of pace. Chairs and tables, umbrellas and planter boxes spill out of doorways, gobbling up the footpath. A bicycle courier with a blue ponytail swerves to avoid an open car door, his green cling suit scalloped with sweat. Beth loves the technicolour tumble of the thoroughfare. She could sit here for hours, eavesdropping on life laid open as customers negotiate business deals and private affairs while they guzzle coffee and graze newspapers, talking into mouthpieces clipped to shirtfronts and coiled around ears, callipered by the gadgets of connection.

She is relieved to have beaten Dale to the cafe and casts an eye over the tables, looking for shade and somewhere to park Cuz. She searches for her favourite waiter, the one who ushers her into a chair as if he is berthing a royal barge. He reminds her of her son, Billy, with his wild mop of dark hair and hazel eyes that wink kindness.

Beth turns and her frame catches the cuffed pants of a

waiter she's not met before. The man trips spectacularly in a fountain of froth and expletives.

'Who's looking after this woman?' he yells. 'There should be a curfew for people her age,' he snaps at the barista behind the bar.

Beth is stunned. What is wrong with him? Pity she can bear. Contempt, even, at a pinch. But condescension, never. She wants to squish him into the ground like an ant but outrage overloads her emotional circuitry, shorting the arch rejoinder he has coming.

Dale arrives, looking as if she belongs everywhere that matters, and leads Beth to a table by the door. Chairs grate as patrons squeeze in to make room for the elderly woman and her aluminium apparatus.

'What's going on, Mum? A bit of impromptu street theatre?'

Beth grimaces and brushes her thick white hair behind her ears. The competition for one-line gags in their family is cutthroat.

'I was looking for a table and he tripped on Cuz. What am I supposed to do, attach flashing blinkers and a warning beep like a reversing truck?'

Dale laughs and Beth begins to recover. Her wit is her strength. It sustained her when she was sleep deprived and housebound with small children; when Billy's heroin addiction hollowed them out; when Roy's environmental ideals made him unfashionable.

The waiter comes back, cloth in hand, and Dale orders two strong lattes.

'I'm sorry for before,' he mumbles to Beth. 'It's a very fast place here most mornings.'

'Just think of me as the local speed bump,' she sniffs.

The waiter smiles stupidly, his muscular build advertising an unhealthy obsession with his body. He wipes their table immaculately clean.

'How's Dad?' Dale asks.

Beth pauses at the crossroad of her answer and makes a detour, turning away from her unease at his recent scattiness. There has been enough drama already this morning. 'You know how he gets when he starts a project. Here he is at seventy-eight, the grand pooh-bah of Australian sculpture, and he's overwhelmed by what's at stake.'

'This is the piece for the weather bureau?'

'Yes. He says it's his last commission.'

'He always talks like that. That's what he said when he went to Broken Hill the trip before last,' Dale says brightly. As long as her parents continue as they always have, she feels twenty, not forty.

'We've both been struck by the last gasps lately,' Beth says. 'Tas next-door's trying to talk your father into buying a new car, which of course would see us out. I suggested getting a black hatchback so it can double up as a hearse. Save you and Billy on funeral costs.'

'Enough gallows humour,' Dale orders.

The waiter scuttles past with a dish of water and sets it alongside the fat golden Labrador scratching hungrily at chewing gum on the pavement, sticky from the heat.

'How's the practice?' Beth enquires, slipping into the patter of their weekly catch-up. News of the psychological disorders treated by her daughter lightens the burden of her own affliction.

'Two new cases of anorexia. One's in hospital on a drip. I can never get used to these beautiful girls almost starving to death.'

'It's the boys I worry about,' says Beth, remembering how surprised she had been at her own son's vulnerability.

'You're not the only one. I'm seeing so many boys now, as young as four and five. Boys who they say aren't behaving themselves.'

'And who are "they", might I ask?'

'Mostly teachers.'

Beth snorts. 'All the years I taught, I never expected boys to sit still. I used to make them run around the quadrangle for ten minutes. Then we'd sing "God Save the Queen" full blast and then, only then, would we get to work.'

Dale can't resist a gentle tease. 'You're a hard woman, you know that?'

'Practical, that's all.'

'So what stage is Dad at with his commission?' Her father's work has its seasons, mostly out of whack with those of the household that he visits less, the closer he comes to a sculpture's birth.

'Horizontal mostly. Deep in thought,' Beth says. 'We're at that awful moment of conception. If he gets blocked or goes blank, I'm coming to stay with you.'

They fall into a moment's companionable musing. Beth glances up as two women, not much younger than Dale, settle themselves at the next table, a baby each tucked in capsules with soft toys at their feet and mobiles dangling overhead.

Dale saw them coming and now looks the other way, to the bus stop across the street where she used to wait every morning as a scholarship girl, giddy with prospects. 'I can't believe it's been twenty years since school,' she says softly. 'I was so sure then about who I wanted to be. Now I look back and think how differently I'd do things.'

Beth frowns. She doesn't like her daughter mooching, wearing grooves up and down the hill of what could've been. 'I was probably the same at your age. You look back at life and unpick all sorts of choices and decisions that felt so right at the time. It gets worse, believe me.'

The Unexpected Elements of Love

'What do you regret, Mum?'

'Is this a national day of mourning?' Beth jollies Dale, sidestepping the question of grandchildren. She isn't yet prepared to surrender hope to the basket of regret, because there's still time, surely. When she last broached this subject, Dale raised her drawbridge and starved Beth into meek apology.

Anyway, it's no good talking over the insistent cry that comes from one of the capsules, which stops only when the child is lifted up and attached to a breast, the mother edging her chair to make room for feeding, the snuffling suckle clearly heard. 'We would have been banished to the bathroom if we'd unbuttoned in public,' Beth observes.

'I've been thinking of taking leave from work to go overseas,' Dale announces abruptly.

Beth is careful not to express judgement. 'Where to?'

'Vietnam. China. Some place I've never been.'

Beth lets the news float by. They finish their lattes in a funk that she blames on the waiter who questioned her sea legs, while Dale decides that the last gasps her mother complained of are in danger of becoming infectious.

PENDULOUS DROPS OF rain plonk like tennis balls on the corrugated iron, teasing a city desperate for moisture. Roy loves his roof for its percussive rhythms. In strong winds the sheets lift and strain and gumnuts rattle down its furrows. The building once stabled two Clydesdales owned by the local dairy and Roy has kept the wooden trough and cobbled stone floor to echo their clop. This is his thinking place. Beth calls it his studio. He says it's his shed, that every man needs one. Not one of those prefabricated humpies barely big enough for a wheelbarrow and rake but a barn of a shed, out back and away from the hum of the hearth.

Tas lost the roof off his shed last year when freak gusts of wind ripped through the North Shore at 150 kilometres an hour. Roy thought his roof would be the first casualty and watched from the house as the gale lashed branches like kelp torn back and forth in the ocean's tide. The power went out for two hours and he sat with Beth, holding hands in the darkness. Even she was silenced by fear of the wind's upper hand, and they welcomed the first siren's call as the city staggered to its feet. Trees had fallen on cars and into lounge rooms but the spider's web attached to the eaves of Roy's studio had survived intact.

Tas went bonkers without his shed. A retired council labourer, he now had nowhere to potter and put his loose ends. Roy told him that he had lost his Dreaming. He likes to stir Tas's discomfort with Indigenous culture; Tas cannot see beyond the glue sniffers and truancy rates. He believes Aborigines have to set themselves right. Proving his own fortitude, he erected a new shed, sturdy enough to withstand the kind of tornado that would twirl lumber in the air as lightly as a cheerleader's baton. Beth calls it the bunker and imagines Tas's plans for a moat and turrets. They laugh at Tas and his wife, Doreen, but assume their neighbours even the score down at the bowling club bar.

The Worboys have lived in this street forever, and although they cannot claim Native title, they share next-door's suspicion of the newest arrivals, who fork out millions for working-class cottages. Tas and Doreen come over every year for Christmas drinks and in between times the couples exchange scraps of talk on the stretch of footpath that is common ground. They never squabble about noise or trespassing creepers. If Tas is a stickler for what goes where, Doreen loves flea market clutter. She lights on junk the way some soft-hearted folk bring home strays.

From the window of his studio Roy can see the plastic rainbow-striped chaise lounge where Doreen sunbakes nude. He feels at home with her bedlam, the way it assaults the senses. His own space is overrun with an untidy collection of objects filched from gutters and nature strips on his rambles. A branch etched with fine lines from the tendrils of the vine that once swaddled it lies on the sill. Beside the door stands a perspex pipe sprouting boughs that curl extravagantly. On his desk sits a stone Buddha with a broken nose, which he'd found face down in a Melbourne laneway. The rough stub reminds him somehow of hubris, of how we might all end our days. On one wall hangs a panel of cast-iron lacework decorated with spiky-leafed waratah flowers that Roy salvaged from an inner-city pub torn down to accommodate the monorail. Flakes of sandstone he likes for their shades of copper and amber fill a large pottery plate that Mora slapped up in her wood-fired kiln decades ago.

The act of trawling is a kind of foreplay, just as athletes limber and stretch. Sometimes the texture and shape of things he has pocketed work their way into his sculpture. Above his drafting table is a mosaic of sea-worn glass plucked from the water's edge during holiday trips to the south coast of New South Wales. Beth used to accompany him on his scouting, until the soft sand bogged her down, leaving her no choice but to sit at home reading while he stalked the shore. He never picked up shells. That was children's plunder: they'd fill their buckets with shards of pink and mauve and mother-of-pearl and then lose interest when the colours faded.

Roy can remember when he first noticed plastic washing in amongst the seaweed and driftwood and clumps of knotted fishing line. He took home stumps of nylon rope, orange and cobalt blue, bright as tropical reef coral. He warms to the synthetic contrast with nature's palette, but the older he gets, the more frightened he is by the tide's turn, and his art amplifies this tension. A respected newspaper critic recently dubbed him an environmental fascist. Broken record, more like it.

It is not solely his obsession with the earth's frailty that sets him apart from most other artists. Lately he has found himself losing his words. The panel discussion at last week's seminar on contemporary Australian sculpture left him fraught. He had taken a question from a young woman in a purple tie-dyed singlet and a skerrick of denim skirt.

'Could you tell me why your recent work, "Bar Code Use By", commercialises the viewer with its electronic scanner. Haven't you adopted the very technology you've always mocked?' she asked earnestly.

'Yes,' Roy said. His mind swam; his mouth was dry. He was thinking of his age, seventy-eight, of where he started, as young and bold as she. He tried to frame an answer but the words kept slipping away and he couldn't get a sentence to stand up on its own. He watched his clumsiness stifle the room. He heard a smatter of coughs and the rustling of papers in the draught from the ceiling fans. Ice cubes clinked as a panel member filled up his glass.

'I find that as I grow older, I need to learn new languages to make myself heard. That's all,' he said finally, winding up questions from the floor.

Afterwards, Roy joined his old friend Morris, a man who could talk small or heavy and after a lot of drink would sing until any gathering forgot plans for an early night. Had anyone noticed his slump, Roy worried, as Morris accompanied him to post-seminar refreshments at the university bar. He tried to follow conversations, to chip in with his bob's worth, but the ideas and interjections outflanked him. He kept his mouth full of wine and food until there was an excuse for mental grogginess.

'You all right?' Morris asked, as they headed for the car park afterwards.

'I went blank,' Roy confessed. 'When that girl asked me a question, I couldn't connect the title with anything.'

Morris shrugged, unconcerned. 'Has this ever happened before?'

Roy wished it had. Perhaps then he'd be able to discount this episode, as he does his occasional bouts of back pain. Familiarity would temper his fear.

Today he swats away the drone of insecurity and busies

himself with plans for the sculpture. The commission is controversial. There is envy from other artists, as always. And some in the media see an agenda in bureau chief Phillip Bennett's choice of an artist long known for taking a provocative stance on ecological issues. Bennett is constantly calling on the government to give him stronger back-up, heftier munition in his fight against global warming. Roy can understand why Bennett panics; he, too, hears disturbances in the world, in the weather.

As a boy, Roy had shied from contemplating the image of the earth rotating in space. Thinking on infinity could paralyse him. 'Mountains out of molehills,' his mother would mutter, irritated by a child she could not indulge while keeping house for a brood of eight and a husband who spent months away from home, surveying the contours of land too rough and lonely for his family to endure.

If anything, age has only honed Roy's sensitivity. He has waking dreams that the poles are melting. He hears of whales stranded on beaches in their hundreds and wonders that people can't read nature's scrambled rhythms. City dwellers in office towers make no link between rain and haymaking, the four-day outlook nothing more than a guide to short sleeves or long. Their thermostats are fixed, but Roy wants to make them sweat, wake them to the glacier's crack at altitudes once silent. He churns out working drawings for his sculpture, in cartoon-hot colours. Their lunacy keeps him entertained for hours on end.

Evening grey has dimmed the room and he switches on the overhead lamp clipped to the back of his chair. He built this chair at university – it's his first living sculpture, a work he is forever adapting. It reclines for reading and rest. It has cushioning for back support and arms broad enough to accommodate sketchpads and books and a mug. He had retreated to it, in a foetal huddle, when he failed second-year architecture and lost his scholarship, and for years it was the only piece of furniture that accompanied his drift through the scruffy inner-Sydney terraces he shared with friends and blow-ins, many of whom have now gone to dust, like the buildings they inhabited.

He hears the car horn sound three times out front, Dale's signal for Beth's homecoming, and leaves his possie to aid his gorgeous woman on her slow procession inside.

JANET HAS CHASED dandelion clocks since she was a child, catching the puffs of seed in cupped hands for as long as it takes to make a wish. That a mature-age woman might be spotted leaping after a floating sphere does not deter her pursuit of one being swept along by a hot northerly. She reaches for it, but just outside her gate it lifts out of reach.

Inside the letterbox is a postcard in her sister Cassie's laboured hand, which begins with 'Dear Snoopy'. Cassie has always said that Janet asks too many questions.

She quickly checks for Cassie's whereabouts, relieved to learn that her sister won't be landing on their doorstep tonight. Tucking the card into her bag, she bends to pick up the tennis balls and one of Harry's school socks that make a trail to their front door. Wet towels greet her in the hallway, followed by the blare of the television, which she switches off, cross at the nanny's disregard for her number one commandment: no TV after school.

'I've got to run, late for class,' Jasmin says airily as she grabs her denim jacket and backpack and makes for freedom. She is studying event management. 'That's her major,' Janet tells friends. 'But she's doing a crash course in chaos theory at our place.'

Jasmin ducks her head back into the kitchen with a post-script. 'Oh, by the way, Harry's lost his lunchbox and he has a project on planets. It was due last week.'

The door bangs in parting salute.

'Can you test my spelling?' Mel asks, emerging from her room.

'Where's Harry?'

'Outside.'

Janet consults the list of words carefully scribed by the girl who had been the first in her class to wrestle with the unforgiving medium of ink. She picks the trickiest noun. 'Accommodation.' While Mel confidently arranges the letters, Janet peers through the kitchen window, bemused at the sight of Harry bent over a watering can, mixing selections from her spice rack, bottles of olive oil and balsamic vinegar, and aftershave from the bathroom cabinet.

'Next word,' Mel prompts, seeing her mother's distracted gaze.

'Expectation.' Janet reaches out to catch a hug from Harry as he shoots inside and heads for the pantry. He pulls free and dives for a canister on the bottom shelf.

'Whoopsie!' he cries, as rice cascades across the floor. He darts back outside clutching packets of noodles for his home-made potion.

'Next word,' Mel pleads, but Janet begins sweeping up the mess. 'Exhaustion,' she improvises.

The phone's ringing brings Harry barrelling back inside, desperate to be the first to grab the handset. Disappointed, he passes the receiver to Janet. It's the video shop – two DVDs overdue. Harry returns to his alchemy, a viscous brew that he stirs before tipping a generous taste into the cat's bowl.

Janet smiles at the industry that eludes him at school. Last week his teacher, Miss Dobbin, had asked if Harry had a kidney problem. 'He's always going to the bathroom. He must have gone eleven times in one afternoon.' She wrinkled her brow and corrected herself. 'Make that twelve. And the last time, he didn't bother coming back to class. The PE teacher found him climbing ropes in the gym.'

The phone rings again.

'Where are you?' Nick asks.

'Home.'

'Home?'

Janet searches the wall calendar to see where else she should be. 'Whoopsie.' There it is, asterisked with a gold star: 7.30 p.m. at the local Indian. Dinner together, every once in a while, had been their New Year's resolution.

'I'll get takeaway,' Nick sighs. 'You find the candelabra.'

Janet laughs and races upstairs to surprise him with a showing of the lingerie he gave her for Christmas. The pink lace bra cuts into her ribcage as Mel screams from below.

Harry has emptied the watering can over his sister's head.

'I hate him,' she shrieks. 'It's stinging me.'

'She wouldn't drink my cordial,' he screams.

'Get to your room,' Janet orders.

She soothes her daughter before going out to inspect Harry's apothecary. Mixed with the shampoo and seasonings are laundry bleach and snail killer from the back shed.

Nick arrives home just as Janet is hauling Harry to his room, where he slams the door and opens it and slams it again until Nick grabs the handle to hold it shut and there is quiet before a second wind sends his soccer ball into the wall, daring them to a fresh duel. Bang, bang, bang, bang. Janet can't stand the relentless pounding, which follows her outside as she cleans up ingredients in the dark. Grabbing scissors from the kitchen, she enters Harry's room and swipes the ball, puncturing it with a single furious stab. The horror on his face as he witnesses her violence is mirrored back at him before she turns to go.

Nick and Janet eat their beef vindaloo out of cartons with plastic forks. Emotionally exhausted, they do not talk. The original deal they'd struck for their irregular romantic dinners had outlawed conversations about the children, but tonight there is nothing else they can possibly discuss.

Remembering Cassie's postcard, Janet pulls it from her bag, which is still slumped against the kitchen bench. 'Cassie's dropped us a line,' she tells Nick, and reads out loud the first sentence her sister has sweated to print neatly. '"Hi guys, I am in Kiama."'

'Christ,' Nick says. 'That's down the bloody road. It's less than three hours drive from here.'

His alarm is part of the pantomime that precedes Cassie's visits. Janet loves her sister. Since their mother died, she and Nick have become an emergency rescue service, answering the reverse-charge phone call that can come at any hour, inheriting the worry of wondering where Cassie's got to; pulling her out of tight spots, finding a bed at a moment's notice. Helping her to make ends meet.

Janet flips the card over to show Nick the photograph of Kiama's main attraction – a giant blowhole spitting a great gob of salty water high over rocks – before continuing the travelogue. '"I'm on my way to Darwin. I'll send you my address when I get settled."'

'That'll be the day,' Nick grunts, no less gratified than Janet to hear that Cassie will be putting distance between them. Their shame, fleeting.

'"I found a gold locket on the beach today. Jackpot! It's

real old, with squiggly initials that I can't make out. Love to everybody. Cassandra.'"

'She should probably have handed the locket in to the police,' Nick notes shortly.

'Finders, keepers, that's her rule.'

Janet can't help admiring Cassie's ingenuity, the way she supplements her disability pension by hoovering beaches with a metal detector after dusk, raking over whatever the day-trippers and sunbakers have left behind. An old flak jacket holds her takings. 'Beachcomber' is what she calls herself, when people ask.

Nick yawns and begins to clean up their leftovers while Janet slides the postcard into an album that records her sister's crisscrossing of the continent, always by bus, because the fares are cheap and Cassie can usually wangle herself the back seat or extra leg-room if she knows the driver, which she usually does. They remember her; she sets her compass by them.

Later in bed, Nick spoons his body against hers and she stiffens in rebuff. Too tired. Undiscouraged, he strokes her, willing them a gentler exit from the evening. Their pleasure offers the briefest reprieve. Nick drifts into sleep but she cannot settle, pecked at by the reminder of Cassie, the sense that something about Harry is not quite right. His shock at her murdering the ball will sit alongside the image she carries of him as a toddler, crying for her and reaching his arm through the pickets of the fence when she left him with the agency nanny, who kept her son clean and fed, but did not fool him for a moment.

ROY OPENS THE fridge for the third time, conducting a forensic search for the beef pie he brought home this morning from the deli. He looks in the fruit and vegetable drawer and scoops out a dead bean and two limp carrots. He feels around the bottom shelf beside the three stubbies of Victoria Bitter that Tas left behind when next-door came over for Christmas drinks. He pushes aside jars of mayonnaise and hot mango pickle and finds a small tub of cream cheese, which on inspection proves to have exceeded its use-by date. He turfs the cheese and stands back against the kitchen bench. Perhaps the cardboard box containing the pie is camouflaged inside the almost empty fridge. He and Beth graze sparingly now that they burn so little fuel. Meanwhile, every item on the supermarket shelf gets bigger. Hens' eggs are jumbo sized. The chocolate bars could feed a boarding school. You buy one thing and score for free something you don't want or need.

'Where did I put the darn thing?' he mutters. After working

all day, he'd intended a night off cooking. Takeaway is a treat he can't enjoy without first begging dispensation from his Scottish Presbyterian forebears, who would have spurned such extravagance. Growing up with seven siblings, he had learnt to slice the loaf thinly and as the baby of the family he'd made do with relics of clothing even the church would have binned for rags.

Roy hears Beth clumsily adjust the volume on the nightly news – remote controls are not designed for the swollen knuckles that barnacle her hands. He takes her in a bowl of olives, an act that arouses suspicion.

'Are we having guests?'

'Not tonight,' he mouths soundlessly.

'Pardon?' She leans forward to catch words that have not been spoken.

A wicked trick and she cottons on, laughing at herself for falling for it again. 'That's not fair, Roy Worboys. You know I can't afford to lose another faculty.'

'Don't talk to me about losing things. I bought us a pie from the deli when I went to the library before, but I can't for the life of me find it.'

'Now, if you were a pie, where would you hide?' Beth asks in her teacher's singsong voice, making a game of his domestic blindness. 'What about the car?' she says, and he pats his pockets, thankful for the jingle of keys that so often go missing. Beth positions her walking frame for upward leverage. 'I'll join the search party. Have you tried the fridge?'

He strokes her hair and kisses the tip of her nose, grateful for her first-class disposition. Not a crackle of irritability evident, which is why children lap her up. She scans kitchen clutter that she would have once cleared away as she swept from room to room, scooping up runaway tea towels, scraps of paper, sticky tape, scissors, mugs bottomed by a swish of cold brown liquid. She can hear Roy's frustration in his trudge to the car port and wonders whether he drove off from the deli with the pie sitting on the roof of the car. She did that once with her wallet.

Aunty Connie was the last member of the family to misplace a dinner. The guests had turned her house upside down, hunting for the meat she swore she had bought. As pre-dinner drinks became the main course, a tipsy hilarity infiltrated proceedings. Beth remembers looking in the laundry basket with her younger sister, Stephanie, who collapsed giggling, smothering her snorts in armfuls of Connie's stockings and generously sized underwear.

They had dined on tomato sandwiches and when Connie went to fetch a tray of ice-cream for dessert, she found the beef frozen solid. No one had thought to check the freezer.

Beth decides not to remind Roy of the night known in her family as 'steak ta ta', in memory of her aunt's senility. She opens the freezer. No pie, but wedged between the ice blocks is a bottle of vodka that Billy has left behind.

Roy heads back in from the car port empty handed. He retraces his movements. 'I stopped to talk to that woman with the yappy Maltese terrier.'

'Mrs Smithers,' Beth prompts. 'Must have been an armed hold-up.'

'You're right. I got stuck and you weren't there to rescue me.'

'Who did?'

'A tall man in a baseball cap with an enormous dog. Great Dane, I think. Huge thing. It sent the terrier into a frenzy and what's her name . . .'

'Mrs Smithers.'

'Snatched up her ball of fluff and practically galloped down the street.'

Beth laughs. Roy sits down beside her on the couch and closes his eyes.

'A pie for your thoughts,' she says, taking his hand.

He gently caresses her fingers; her thin gold wedding band is in-grown after forty-five years of wear. Roy has clung to the lustre of youth, his olive complexion still fresh, cropped silvery hair, attractive in his signature black T-shirts and jeans. From the shoulders up, Beth has aged just as graciously. She has steel-grey eyes and a strong face that holds its character even as the skin loosens around her neck and cheekbones. In sickness and in health – Roy thinks of the vow they have honoured, their achievement eclipsing the marvel of living beyond a hundred in a world where loyalty is harder to win than new hips or a fortified heart.

The rain has stopped but water drips from the eaves, tick-tocking in the darkness. Through the open window they can hear the sounds of the street, the tap of Jack Mangan's walking stick and the sniff and scamper of his beagle Rex on their nightly stroll to the corner and back. Beth knows the neighbourhood's habits. When she was young her father took the family on sabbatical to Washington for a year. On summer evenings, neighbours sat on the stoop while Beth and her sister played with Sally Kozwalski who lived two doors down, catching fireflies in old jam jars. Beth visited the street with Roy thirty years later and could see little trace of her memories of scruffy congeniality in the decorative spruce of gentrification, the polished brass plates on enamelled gloss doors. The houses were air-conditioned and families no longer sat on the steps craving a breeze.

Last Christmas she'd had a card from Sally, with a newspaper clipping about a man their age who had lived on their street and died in his sleep. A considerable time had lapsed between his death and the discovery of his body, which had lain rotting in his bed until two Jehovah's Witnesses came knocking. They deduced from the putrid odour and pile of mail lying on the mat that the occupant was past saving, and they called the police. The story has been preying on Beth. She's assembling evidence that testifies to neglect of the elderly and is alarmed at the weight of it.

Mora had posted her an item downloaded from the Internet, flaunting her technological prowess. The snippet announced that granny dumping was on the rise. The term was coined after an 82-year-old woman had been left by her daughter-in-law at an airport, parked by a window where she was found two days later drenched in urine. The stench gave her away. Beth is amazed that people can go missing in crowds. She wrote back to Mora, in fountain pen on parchment, telling her of a Japanese experiment in which microchips were inserted into the armpits of elderly people to keep track of their movements.

Beth does her bit, calling on Angie who is ninety-six and lives alone in a weatherboard five doors down, which is being swallowed whole by morning glory vine. Angie is grateful for the attention – the council has contracted home meals to a firm that leaves trays on the doorstep and instructs staff to decline invitations for refreshments or a 'while you're here, there's a light bulb needs changing'.

Beth's experience at the cafe is further proof that old age is a turn-off. Once it was children who were not heard. Now toddlers are treated to baby cappuccinos and buckets of toys. Capitalism values their trade but an elderly customer is worse than finding a black wiry hair in your lemon sorbet. Bugger that, Beth thinks. People campaign for tuna, battery hens and old-growth forests, but Greypeace doesn't have quite the zing of its environmental counterpart. Still, if scientists are forbidden by law from experimenting on monkeys, then waiters should at least treat elders with deference. She's going to write a letter to the local paper.

She wants to tell Roy but he's fallen asleep in front of a two-hour special on the last Bee Gees. She can't see a pen and paper within reach and doesn't want to wake him after the evening's culinary mishap. Instead, she closes her eyes and composes a masterly piece of barbed prose in her head.

TOO HOT TOO early, and after a night that stifled breath.

'Janet?' Nick yells from the laundry, where he is looking for the black shoe polish, but all he hears in return is the shudder of water pipes as she starts her shower. Surveying the chaos of the shelves, he thinks of the girlfriend who mothered him through med school, washing his clothes, ironing his shirts and even his boxer shorts, cocooning him in the haven that he wishes sometimes he had preferred over the squall that is his wife.

He finds the polish in the crate of gardening tools and is surprised to see that it has melted in the tin, the metal warm to touch. He applies too much and manages to brush a charcoal smudge across his fine white wrist.

He has two embryo implants this morning. Both couples are desperate: the technology that has delivered gratification to so many others has failed them thus far. Sometimes Nick thinks that the task of telling people they cannot conceive a life is worse than disclosing the shadow of death. He watches frustration, then grief, weather faces; he can only guess at the layers of loss beneath.

Dale Worboys is Nick's first appointment this morning. She'd read about his fertility clinic in an article on reproductive tourism. The very next day she arranged a meeting. The two-week wait became interminable, which was ridiculous given twenty years of putting off a decision she had never expected to make on her own. Sitting across from him at his desk, she is glad for his crispness as he steps through the preliminaries: her age, her cycles, reproductive history; sperm donors, his background, services the clinic provides.

'Why've you left it so late?' he asks.

'I was away the day we learnt about family planning,' she bats back, glad for Nick's laughter. 'I just expected this part of my life to fall into place. I still hope it will.'

'Hang on to your hope. It's your oxygen tank.'

'You sound like my mother.'

'I'm taking that as a compliment.' He guesses from her grey silk suit and stately bearing that she is handsomely off. 'I want to warn you at the very beginning that this could be long and fraught and you might walk out of here empty handed.'

Surprised by his directness, Dale takes a moment to gather what is left to her. 'I'm a fatalist at heart, so I guess if I try and don't succeed, I won't die wondering. I'll get on with life. I'm a psychologist. I love my job, but not like some people. I'd happily give up work to raise a family. Happily,' she repeats. 'I want to love someone more than myself. I just don't want to be alone any more.' She raises an eyebrow at Nick, half humorously. 'You must be tired of hearing this story.'

Sometimes the hollow knock of emptiness sounds in his room all day. He checks his notes. She's forty-two, the same age as his wife. 'You have a whisker of time left. That's all. There's no getting around your age.'

Dale clutches her handbag. 'I've been swotting up and I know the odds give me no cause for joy.' Conversational levity is a coping mechanism she's learnt from Beth, useful on occasions such as this.

'If you choose insemination, it's a simple enough procedure, about as uncomfortable as a pap smear. You have a ten per cent chance of a pregnancy per cycle. There's an even lower likelihood of delivering a healthy baby through IVF.' No tears, he thinks, but the quiver of her chin suggests they're not far beneath the surface. 'I suggest we book you in for a screening and go from there.'

He wants her to take home a possibility, for tucking under her pillow. 'Don't feel that you're a lost cause, Dale, because this journey is worth taking.'

For the first time she flutters with excitement. 'You have children?'

'Two kids. One's easy. One's a nightmare. I'd love to have a couple more.'

'Tell me about the nightmare.'

Nick hesitates. 'You most probably have enough troubled kids and their parents queuing at your door every day.'

Dale is undeterred. 'Like I said, I love my work.'

'It's our son, he's a livewire, always in trouble at school, over anxious.'

She's intrigued. 'Anxious about what?'

'Storms mainly,' Nick says, sorry now that he has opened up this much.

'Weather can be frightening. I wouldn't want to experience a cyclone like the one that just hit up north.'

'Sure, but Harry's tuned in to changes in the weather that most of us wouldn't notice. A strong wind unsettles him.'

Dale could see Nick tensing up. 'He probably has one fewer skin than the rest of us. Why should that be a red flag?'

'Well, he hyperventilates sometimes, if the weather's wild.'

'Does this worry you?'

'Off and on.' He shrugs. 'We sometimes beat ourselves up about our parenting but at least we have a control group, our daughter, and she's fine.' He doesn't mention other aspects of Harry's behaviour that prey on him, embarrassed that he'd temporarily forgotten who's consulting whom.

But Dale seems unfussed. 'I once treated a girl, she was

six, and she'd only eat white food. Rice, potatoes, chicken breast. Fear of thunder strikes me as being more rational than a fear of carrots. Another of my patients stopped swallowing because he was terrified of choking. You'll be glad to hear both children are perfectly normal. Look, why don't I give you my card?' She takes one from a silver case in the pocket of her jacket and hands it to Nick. 'If you decide to seek help for your son, maybe I can recommend someone.'

As she straightens to depart, she catches sight of a small rusty sign propped up against the bookcase behind his desk.

'A present from my wife.' Nick rolls his eyes as Dale laughs at the advertisement for 'Fresh Eggs'. 'An eccentric sense of humour,' he explains. 'You know, the funny thing about Harry's fear of storms is his mother. She's a weather presenter on cable television.'

Dale stares at him closely as she puts the pieces together.

JANET HOPS OUT of the shower and regards herself in the mirror. She has spent more time wondering what to wear to her appointment with Dale than ordering her thoughts about Harry. She missed the last reunion of their matriculation year but had received a thorough debriefing from Anna, the one schoolfriend she still sees, at their monthly book club. Anna can read a woman's life story by the cut of her clothes and the jut of her chin. She's the kind of woman Janet sometimes catches herself longing to be – home, and hummingly happy to be there. Anna wasn't impressed by Dale's aloneness: no husband or partner or offspring, and no sign that she was pursuing opportunities, either. Dale has two cats and that's all, Anna reported.

Dale is smart, thinks Janet, stooping to pick up the plastic milk bottles Harry's used as skittles, turning the hallway into a bowling alley. The cleaners are coming and, perversely, she spruces the house before the Korean husband-and-wife team arrive with vacuum cleaners strapped to their backs like rocket boosters.

She is flying now, top on toothpaste, tampons back in the cabinet, Mel's book in her room, Harry's tennis ball in his, a lost sock into the laundry basket, Nick's jogging shorts, dirty pantyhose, fling, fling, fling, moving so fast she nicks her hip on the edge of the wardrobe and is cursing and rubbing its sting when Nick's shout echoes up the stairs.

'I'm off.'

'Bye,' she sings out. 'I'll ring you later.'

She steps into a sleeveless navy blue dress and grabs a tailored red jacket for her air-conditioned office, where you could freeze to death during a heatwave.

She'd never set out to be on camera. After completing an unremarkable arts degree, she'd landed a job in the meteorological bureau. At first she fielded media calls, before moving on to fill the role of spokeswoman. She surprised herself by being credible and confident in radio interviews and live crosses and had leapt at the offer to take up a role on television. However, she'd been unprepared for the power of the small screen. People she has never met sing out to her, 'What's tomorrow's weather?' As if she can bring on a fine day to please them.

She loves her work. The pay is generous and she is proud of her independence. From as early as she can remember, she was bred to look beyond the compound of home by a mother who was over-educated and under-employed, and ultimately disappointed by marriage.

Sometimes Janet's a little scared, unnerved, by her addiction to the adrenaline rush of meeting deadlines. Mel's arrival had complicated things, but Janet could still move easily enough between the worlds of home and work. Harry's needs, though, make everything a battle. And there is always the guilt: as if reporting on highs and lows matters in the face of quietening the unpredictable waves of family life. Undeterred, she turns up at the studio each day, glad for a leave pass, grateful to win recognition for a job well done.

Now her boss, Harvey, is pressing for steeper audience gains. He wants graphic footage of disasters, of caravan parks being battered by cyclones, people clinging to wreckage. She prefers talking heads, policy analysis, the close scrutiny of political and corporate responses to the warming.

'Infotainment,' Harvey announces with relish, 'is all about sweetening the savoury.' British born, he wears a gold signet ring on his little finger. He calls women 'darlin'', in a niggling challenge to workplace codes of correctness. 'Listen, darlin',' he told Janet yesterday, 'Mr and Missus Stringbag don't want lectures on isobaric surfaces and geostrophic wind speeds. They want to sit in their cosy lounge chairs watching some poor bastard's furniture floating out the door.'

'Miss Stringbag might fancy an explanation,' slipped out

of Janet's mouth. 'And she's the hip Generation Y viewer with heaps of disposable income that the sales department keeps telling us we've got to reach.'

Jenny Monk, sports editor, working mother and Janet's soul mate, wanted to punch the air and holler but every mutiny against Harvey is tamed by their reluctance to upset his thin-lipped tolerance of their flexible hours.

Sometimes during these meetings Janet sits doodling geometric patterns, imagining Harvey slouched on a resort banana lounge with a pineapple daiquiri, oblivious to the waves draining into the belly of an approaching tsunami. But Harvey rarely goes on holidays. In fact he barely goes home. His environment is remote-controlled – he parks his car every morning three floors underground and leaves the building after dark, the window of his expansive corner office just another image next to the bank of television monitors lining his wall.

Janet is as blinkered in her own way as to what goes on around her. Expecting children who pleased and thanked you, who accommodated a complicated, busy existence, she was unprepared for the tremors of a boy who is angry and anxious all at once. She has consulted definitions of neuroses in paediatric texts but the entries peter out after volcanoes, monsters, darkness, dinosaurs and dogs. There is never any mention of a terror of isolated showers. Even as a baby, Harry would start awake at the sound of frangipani branches scratching at his nursery window, lying wide eyed in his cot. When he was three, Nick had to take him home from the kindergarten picnic because he was terrorised by autumn leaves blowing across the concrete courtyard. At four he was scared of coconut palms, imagining their pliant trunks bent double from hurricane-force winds, the high-pitched fury of a tropical storm.

Janet arrives at Dale's office five minutes early and drives around the block twice before snaffling a one-hour park beside a limp bottlebrush growing in a handkerchief of dirt. The heat bears down as she opens the car door. She's come alone, reluctant to cart Harry in for inspection, to magnify foibles and fears that might subside of their own accord.

Dale's building is cool and she climbs the stairs to the third floor, pausing at the second-level landing where the sign welcoming her to Busi-tech Pty Ltd has come loose, its arrow pointing skyward.

In the waiting room a young receptionist with a pierced eyebrow gives Janet a form to fill out. As the only chair has been taken by a painfully thin teenage girl in a school uniform, Janet leans against the counter, ticking boxes and providing health fund numbers. The form asks how she'd heard of Dale's practice, and Janet calculates the degrees of separation. Her intimacy with Dale had been knitted over swapcards and tennis lessons and illicit cigarettes smoked under the Norfolk pine in the park behind school. But Janet had fallen in with a faster crowd, while Dale completed her Duke of Edinburgh medal and became a prefect, distinguishing herself as the girl most likely to go places – mountaintops or international capitals, but not the quiet of this office. Janet hears the clip of heels and sees Dale coming towards her, arms outstretched.

'You look great,' Dale says, giving her a quick hug.

'On the outside.'

'You've come to the right place then,' Dale jokes.

Janet is impressed by her ease. 'Anna said she saw you at the reunion.'

'Well, I see you all the time on the tele, and then last week you were on the back of a bus. There I was, stuck in traffic staring at this photo of you, and I thought, Janet didn't have half as many blackheads as that at school.'

Janet roars. She had forgotten how Dale made her laugh. Forgotten, too, her tidiness. Always wholesomely pure, apart from the tints in her short bobbed hair.

For all their years apart, they remain slaves to the same fashion code. Janet admires Dale's tailored poise as she is ushered into a sunlit room. Colourful crayon drawings hang higgledy piggledy on the walls. Janet scans them for signs of distress but the spidery stick figures need an interpreter.

Dale follows her gaze. 'When I first saw David's picture of his family it took me a while to realise that his father was missing. He told me that his dad spends a lot of time in the garage.'

'How's your famous father?' Janet asks, taking her cue from the glass sculpture sitting on a small table.

'Mum's almost crippled with arthritis, so Dad's the house husband. They're an amazing pair. I marvel at how my parents have been there for each other, and for us.'

'They're lucky.'

'It's more than luck. More than love, even. It's made of something stronger. Sometimes I think marriage is like stone masonry, a dying craft.'

Janet nods and takes notepad and pen from her briefcase, her pacifiers. She squeezes a balled-up tissue in one hand as she leads Dale through the story of Harry.

MISS DOBBIN CLAPS a rhythmical sequence for the third time this morning and the twenty-six and a half children (Brendan was only half there, she once confided to her mother) copy it back, mangling the rhythm. It's time to dispense the medication for those students with Attention Deficit Hyperactivity Disorder.

'Matthew,' she says firmly, 'keep your hands to your own body.'

She's scratchy today, after a late night with a stopwatch and whistle, timing contestants at the school swimming carnival. Afterwards a group of teachers kicked on with a cask of wine and a floorshow by the sportsmaster, a legendary mimic.

The children seem tired, too, and the hot north wind stirring straws and cellophane across the basketball court will soon infiltrate the classroom. She scans the timetable. Art will be the first lesson after lunch, a licence for her class to misbehave under the guise of creative expression.

Last week they had started making their papier-mâché masks. Harry had glued Claire Bunting's plaits together with flour and water paste that ended up all over everywhere. Today they will be painting faces on the casts, their knees and any other surface begging adornment. The boys rarely wear protective smocks, which they conveniently forget to bring or remember to lose.

'Right,' she says. 'Rodney, Michael, Damien and Brendan, come out the front and the rest of you get your lunchboxes. Quietly,' she adds, pointlessly, as they scramble for their bags. 'Twenty house points for anybody who puts more food in their mouth than on the floor.'

'Good girl, Tilly,' she says to a girl she pegs as one certain to turn into a troublemaker in due course – nobody can go through life being this compliant. Tilly Sanders sits at her desk unwrapping a small plastic parcel of celery sticks. You can picture the state of a child's home by the state of their lunchbox, Miss Dobbin tells her mother almost daily. Tilly's lunch is full of crunch, she rhymes to herself. Rice crackers. Peanuts. Carrots. Earnestly healthy. Peter Gilmore orders a sausage roll and chocolate milk from the school canteen every day of the week. Her initial guess that he lives with a single mother who works full-time was hopelessly off beam. Dad is in charge, and Miss Dobbin likes the look of him. She is making discreet enquiries to flesh out the family's history.

The Unexpected Elements of Love

Jane Arnold's lunch is homemade; the fruit comes in a paper napkin with a biblical quotation and a smiley face. Today's is from Genesis. 'Come, let us build ourselves a city, and a tower with its top in the heavens.'

Rodney, Michael, Damien and Brendan are fidgeting with the rubber bands on her desk, itching to nab them for combat. She hands each boy a marshmallow that contains milligrams of a drug she describes to her mother as 'my little helper'. The marshmallow is meant as a decoy but everybody in the class, and their parents, know which kids take a daily tablet.

The sudden slam of the heavy wooden door startles her and the absolute silence that follows suggests the children have been knocked off centre, too. But when they register that the wind is the culprit, their giggling moves through the classroom like a Mexican wave. Harry sits still, eyes large in his small face. Matthew props the door open again, in the hope of an encore. 'Boom,' shrieks Brendan, skinny arms flapping with excitement.

'What if Mr Breen was coming in, and "bang!"' Tommy slaps his hand into his head and rolls his eyes and Miss Dobbin knows instinctively that the mirth and silliness will spread as they hallucinate the nuisance that a wind can cause. Tommy, freckled from forehead to toe, is learning classical piano but his skills as a ham suggest the club circuit as a lucrative fallback. This year's Year 2 is freaky for its share of difficult children, most of them boys.

Some days she yearns for the precocity of the gifted girls in the extension class she took last year at a private school. Take yesterday for starters. She spent an hour after the last bell supervising Angus and Harry, who had been ordered to scrub the school bus after they were caught splattering it with rotten fruit from the bins. The teacher on duty said the boys had been almost quivering with exhilaration.

But now Harry sits rocking, his eyes turned anxiously to the overcast sky. He stands, spellbound by the clouds, and stumbles as he catches his toe on a pint-sized wooden chair. The rest of the class packs away crusts and chip packets, rearing to play outside, but Harry leans against the window, pressing his cheek to the glass to get a better look at the ash-coloured sky. The wind thwacks the venetian blinds and another grand slam shivers the classroom. The shock shanghais Miss Dobbin out of her chair.

'Lunchboxes in bags. Pick up every scrap of paper and plastic wrap and peel and line up at the door in single file. Quietly.'

She turns to find Harry crouching beside his desk, his eyes riveted by the slow-moving drama of atmospheric drift. 'What's wrong, Harry?'

He wipes his big brown eyes with the back of a grubby hand, his right leg jiggling with the effort of holding back tears. 'Is it going to rain?' he whispers.

'What did you say?' She cocks her head and draws closer to his mouth.

'Is it going to rain?'

Miss Dobbin frowns, bemused by the sudden timidity of this child who has distinguished himself as her most challenging, a word she remembers to use in conversation with the principal. At home with her mother, she does not mince words. Harry, she says, is a handful.

A crack in the sky answers Harry's question and he quakes. While Miss Dobbin sighs at a challenge that is beyond the perimeter of her lesson plan.

BETH COULD SIT in the shower for hours, letting the warm water shoo away her pain, if only the hot water service would oblige. Roy had scavenged a plastic chair from a pile of hard rubbish and carted it home for her to use in the recess. Her mother used to joke that she had been a fish in a previous life; as a young child Beth would peel off her clothes at every opportunity, to feel the splash of water on skin. The day Stephanie was christened, she'd wandered into the garden of the manse next door and was found wading in the murky fishpond, her best white dress laced with algae.

Shrouded by steam, she turns off the taps and contemplates her tortured limbs. An hour from now she will be in harness at her weekly Pilates class. Dale bought her a shiny turquoise leisure suit as a joke, and Beth insists on wearing it. Anyone who dares a second glance gets told that she's off to aerobics, frame and all.

Roy has been mettlesome this morning. In the kitchen she'd strained to hear what he was saying to himself over the clatter of cutlery thrown into the drawer. His soliloquy of discontent was familiar. Aunt Connie used to mutter like that, a *sotto voce* conversation with herself, listing grievances like a prayer. By day's end her voice would be shrill and gale-forced, hitting out at everything and anyone. Once, on a family outing in a crowded train carriage, she had defaced her mouth with a bright red lipstick stripe, in a rage of self-hate.

Beth brushes her hair and hears Roy accounting for his keys, glasses and wallet in the leather satchel he takes everywhere. The most quotidian excursion now involves the kind of baggage check associated with overseas departure.

Roy backs their small car clear of the car port and pulls up outside their sandstone cottage, which has a fence but no gates. They'd got rid of them when the energy expended in letting themselves in and out exceeded their faith in the burglar deterrence gates might afford. As for the valuables tucked in bottom drawers, Beth's pleasure in them is diluted by her grandmother's philosophy that one should enjoy objects without wanting to own them.

Watching Beth shuffle down the path, Roy thinks of the helium-filled, slow-motion gait of astronauts in space, and he smiles at the prospect of sharing the image with his wife. They have joked that John Glenn's return to space at seventy years of age was a test run for resettling geriatrics by the rocket load to another planet.

Roy opens the door for his wife and she lowers herself into the car while he folds up Cuz and stows it in the boot.

'Oh hell,' Beth says, as Roy gets into the driver's seat and shuts the door.

'What's the matter?'

'I've left a letter inside that I want to post.'

Roy stares at her in disbelief.

She humours him as he prepares to retrace his steps. 'Well, at least your legs work.'

He finds an envelope on the kitchen table, addressed in Beth's fluent script to the editor of the *North Sydney Times*. Out of habit he checks that the back door is locked, just in case the question comes into dispute two sets of traffic lights down the road.

Roy takes the back streets, refusing to be hurried by the European car sniffing at his bumper. Beth ticks him off. 'You'll get us both shot in an attack of road rage.'

'There's Celia.' Beth waves as Roy slows, looking for a park close to the Crowther Centre for Health and Wellbeing. Celia is trying to repair cartilage damaged from years of ballet mistresses pushing her to the brink. Now twenty-six, she is beautifully proportioned, with that mix of strength and fragility that distinguishes dancers from athletes. Everything about her is graceful, except for the crewcut. She walks with her toes turned outwards, and when she bends from the waist her hands sweep the floor and her forehead brushes her knees.

Celia and Beth nurse their ailments sunnily. They have more in common than a glance would suggest. For one thing, they both love fudge caramels, which neither can eat. Beth abstains because her teeth crumble at the slightest provocation. Celia avoids sugar and fat because of the flab these lovelies slap on her thighs. They began Pilates on the same day over a year ago and their instructor dubbed them Bib and Bob, until he came up with better nicknames. Beth now answers to Goldilocks, because of her chutzpah, and Celia is known as Thongs, because she can flip-flop like no one else. Sharing coffees after the first class, they christened their teacher The Rack, which stuck. His sobriquets are meant to butter up his victims before they turn against him on the long march towards rehabilitation. Beth, however, doesn't bother with the illusion of recovery. She just wants to hold the gangrene at garter level.

Celia floats up to the car to assist with Beth's disembarkation. Beth smells tobacco on her breath as they exchange pecks on both cheeks.

It always takes Celia a minute to adjust to Beth's laboured pace. The Rack once compared them to a kid goat skipping on the spot beside a bogged water buffalo. His directness doesn't suit everybody. He says in his defence that growing a thick hide is part of the Pilates therapy. Beth threatens to take him to the war crimes tribunal.

Inside, The Rack is impatient to begin. Raphael, the gay circus performer who usually joins the girls after class for coffee, salutes as they enter. He dislocated his shoulder doing gratis stuntwork for a friend's low-budget film and the reconstructive surgery has left him sore and doubtful. The Rack calls him Arnie, as in Schwarzenegger, because of his brawn, which clashes with his hairless chest and colourful, feminine accessories; he wears silk vests made from old dressing gowns that he buys from church op shops. Beth nods to Sook, the rugby league player. A mature-age woman, surely too scrawny to have sustained a sporting injury, is introduced to the class as Virginia and later given the name Elbows, in honour, they presume, of her coat-hanger figure. Beth wonders why their tormentor did not go for a blunter nom de plume, like Stalk.

The Rack lulls the group into action with gentle stretches. Raphael grunts and groans without inhibition. Beth is more stitched up. She farts like a schoolboy at home but in public she suppresses her rudeness, unlike Mora who lets one go whenever the urge takes hold. 'You've been on your own too long,' Beth cussed when her friend nearly intoxicated a queue of shoppers at the supermarket checkout.

The new lady emits shallow, breathy squeaks. Beth closes her eyes and concentrates on The Rack's directions. She floats away, thinking of the letter she has written to the local newspaper, and then of Roy, who has gone to the library to chase an article by a Norwegian scientist who argues that the threat of global warming is exaggerated. She worries about his forgetfulness. She half expects the pie to turn up in the linen cupboard, smelling like a bag of prawn shells. At least Roy can laugh at himself. When the doorbell rang last Sunday afternoon, he did not skip a beat. 'That must be Friday night's dinner with its crust between its legs.'

Beth smiled at his joke but she's bothered by his lapses. Roy is more than her morning and her noon. If part of him goes missing, they are both done for: the adage 'less is more' does not apply to the mind. He would take her down with him. Losing her legs has hardened Beth to the practical realities of managing life's descent. 'Shoot me if I fall that far,' she used to tell him on the way home from Aunty Connie's place. Roy had agreed with her, hadn't he?

'Goldilocks?' stamps The Rack on the floor beside her head. 'Asleep on the job, are we?'

'No,' she says, gathering herself. 'I am busy rising from the dead.'

She looks across at Celia and Raphael, both perspiring, concentrating hard. These two are blessed with a faith in healing that is difficult to manufacture at Beth's end of the production line. If she could believe in a cure, or even trick herself that it was possible, she would be sweating, too. It's not that she doesn't believe in mind over matter – she had watched Stephanie conquer breast cancer by taking her recovery for granted. No concession to doubt.

In the cafe where they retreat every week after class, Celia and Raphael order herbal tea. Beth requests a strong latte with full-cream milk, to register her delinquency.

'I'm going to Melbourne tomorrow,' Raphael announces. 'It's Mum's birthday. She's seventy-three.'

'A baby,' says Beth.

They turn to her agog, which is a compliment really. Mesmerised by her conversational dexterity, they'd lost sight of the frame, the shuffle and the white hair.

'How old are you?' Celia asks.

'Seventy-five next month,' Beth says. 'I'm having a rave party. Bring your own ecstasy.'

Celia giggles until a dribble of tea escapes from her mouth and rolls down her chin.

Beth hands her a paper napkin. 'So what are you giving your mum?' she asks Raphael.

'I've made her a shrine. It's really just a collection of things that she loves.' His voice grows quiet, as if he anticipates mockery. 'She's in a nursing home. It's an awful place. Not that she really knows where she is. We don't really know where she is, either. I hate going to see her. I always start off feeling guilty, like we've discarded her. And then, after an hour of sitting there, I start clock-watching and working out when I can nick off. But the moment I leave, I start feeling guilty again.'

'Does she recognise you?' Beth asks, of the fate she fears most.

'Yes and no. She spends most of the time . . .' Raphael buries his face in his hands but when he looks up at them again he is smiling. 'I'm going to laugh at this but I'm not being heartless.' He pauses again. 'Oh God.' He straightens and his lips quiver, as if he might cry. 'She sits there with one of those big, striped carry bags, the red, blue and white reffo bags from two dollar shops, and it's full of other plastic bags and God knows what else, bits of foil wrapper, things she's picked up off the floor or taken from other people's rooms, and she sits riffling through it like she's looking for something she's lost. It's weird, because when we were growing up she was such a tyrant if we ever lost anything. I still remember the day I left my lunchbox on the bus and she made me go all the way to the terminal to track it down. A lunchbox, for God's sake.'

'Won't the shrine end up in her bag?' Celia wonders.

'No, I'm going to hang it on the wall beside the bed. It's made out of a music box and when you open the door it plays the overture from *The Pearl Fishers*. She loves opera, at least she used to.'

'I think it sounds beautiful.' Beth is moonstruck by his

tenderness. But the image he has conjured, of the frightening hairpin bend that she and Roy are approaching, sinks her deep.

She consults her watch. He should be here to pick her up any minute now.

THERE ARE NO parking spots when Roy reaches the library so he circles the block slowly until he is tooted from behind, not once but four times. A young woman in a blue sports car with the roof down gives him the finger. Flustered, he pushes on and is swept into a lane for right-hand turns only, taking him away from the library and towards the highway where traffic is hurtling on to feeder roads for the Sydney Harbour Bridge. He feels like a kayaker heading for the falls; when he sees the sign for an underground parking station, he follows the arrow into quieter waters. He usually avoids tunnels and subways, out of a fear of being trapped. Beth derides his neurosis but he cannot shut down the newsreel in his brain, the vivid pictures of smoke and sandwiched cars, the soundtrack of chaos.

'We live in Sydney, not Los Angeles,' she tells him. Australia is a disaster-free zone in her book, far from the fault lines of trouble.

Roy noses his car down into the bowels of the earth. He hates the tightness of these multi-storey car parks, cheaply built and crudely designed. The pylons at each turn are streaked with duco scabbed off bodies and Roy's chest constricts as he drives from floor to floor looking for a park. But it seems there are none.

A young mother with a screaming baby and an overflowing supermarket trolley approaches a four-wheel drive and Roy decides to wait for her to exit. As she straps the howling toddler into the back seat, her foot nudges the trolley and it rolls away, picking up speed on the downward incline. Roy springs out of his car to arrest the trolley before its prow can slam into a parked car.

The mother is right behind him. 'Thank you so much. These things are feral, aren't they? I always get the one with bung wheels.' She swings the trolley around and pushes it back to her car.

Roy turns back to his. Patting his pocket for the keys, he suddenly chokes with panic. The smart locking system has outwitted him. The engine is idling. The keys hang in the ignition; the doors are locked. His car is at an angle, blocking the departure of the mother and child's four-wheel drive and likely that of the very large lady with a bulging hessian bag who is heading for the stationwagon with the 'Magic Happens' sticker on its back windscreen.

'I'm terribly sorry,' Roy splutters to the mother. 'I've locked my keys in the car.'

'Oh shit.' Her voice is thin with disappointment at this latest snare. 'Perhaps you'd better call roadside service.'

'Yes, of course. Do you have a phone?'

She dials the number for him and passes him the phone.

'They can take hours,' drawls the large woman as she opens the door of her wagon and squeezes into the driver's seat with its threadbare lamb's wool cover; lolly wrappers litter the floor.

For the second time this morning Roy feels at the mercy of an undertow sucking him along. He is put on hold and listens to a recorded message system promising that his call is important and will be answered by the first available operator. Citizens know such refrains by heart, just as they used to know the Lord's Prayer.

'Your conversation may be taped and used for training purposes,' a voice explains. 'Listen to the menu and follow the prompt. Press one for membership queries. Press two for insurance. Press three for accounts. Press four for roadside service. If you want to speak to an operator, press zero.'

Roy does as he is told and waits for connection to the operator. A tall man with an aluminium briefcase and dark glasses, realising he is parked in, glares at Roy and exchanges words with the mother, who has taken her little boy out of the car.

The child grips her hand and totters on chubby legs, enthralled by his reflection in all the chrome that surrounds him.

Roy remains on hold.

The graveyard of metal is wakening. A woman in a navy skirt and striped blouse walks towards them, talking on a mobile phone. Her mouth purses when she sees that her exit is blocked. The young mother, who has become master of ceremonies, recounts what has happened, pointing to Roy. The woman in turn relays the event into her phone, consults her watch, then turns back the way she has come. The air is thickening with exhaust and exasperation.

The man with the briefcase is losing patience. 'For Christ's sake.' He shakes his head at the stupid old codger. Pointing his keys at a Jeep, he opens the door, sits inside and takes a palm-sized computer from his briefcase, tapping at its screen with a thin reed.

Distracted by the man's prickliness, Roy registers the voice of the operator too late and yells 'Help!' But she has moved on to the next caller. Desperate now, he takes the phone to the mother and knows from the way she grabs it and redials the number that her kindness has been stretched and she is hardening towards the view that he is too old to be out on his own. God smiles on her promptly, and she arranges for a service van to meet him out the front.

Roy thanks her and she points him in the direction of the

lift, but his confidence is shot and his pulse throbs as he stares at the panel of buttons to choose from. S for shops, F for food hall, M for mall, W for walkway. Whatever happened to G for ground? He presses W, making a lateral connection between walking and fresh air, but the doors open to a glass-covered walkway spanning the very four-lane highway that had lured him underground.

It's worse than being lost in the bush, where at least bewilderment has a heroic and honourable tradition. The crackle of a walkie-talkie announces the approach of a cyclist with a blue ponytail, wearing a skin-tight suit and streamlined helmet. Roy appeals for directions but the courier is arguing about a drop-off address with the hissing and spitting speaker in his gloved hand. Roy follows him downstairs, catching sight of the street at one end of the walkway. It's not the entrance to the car park, but he figures he can find that once he steps out into natural light. He passes shopfronts selling plasma screens and spectacles. A travel agency window promises cheap flights to Mozambique. Isn't Mozambique under water? Roy struggles to remember last night's news, or was it a story he read somewhere?

When he reaches the end of the walkway he realises that what he thought was the exit is a cruel trick. There's no door. Only a glass wall. Panicking now, he presses his nose and hands against the tinted glass and there on the other side is the courier. Roy pounds the window to get his attention, until he feels a cool hand on his arm. It is a woman dressed in white. She looks like a nurse or an angel.

'Can I help?'

'The exit,' he says. 'My car has broken down and I have to meet road-service at the entrance to the underground cemetery.' He scrambles to explain what he really means, pleased that he at least recognises his gaffe. 'I need to find the entrance to the underground car park.'

'There are two ways,' the angel says, shifting her cane basket from one arm to the other. She points back the way Roy has come. 'Follow me. We'll go together.'

'Thank you. Thank you.' He has never felt more grateful.

The woman rolls from side to side as she walks and Roy is embarrassed to notice the bunions that have deformed the shape of her white leather shoes. He is breathing more easily now, with the relief of being taken in hand; the building feels friendlier, more secure. The woman chatters as they walk. She is off to lawn bowls and uses the shopping centre as a shortcut. Roy longs for Beth's conversational knack but his tongue is in a wheelchair.

'I had trouble finding a park,' he begins, which sets the woman nodding vigorously in cosy accord.

'Parking spots have gone the way of good manners,' she tuts. 'Rarely find them when you want them, not that I use my car much. Once a week I drive to see my sister, May. She lives on the Central Coast. Here I am spilling the family beans and I haven't even introduced myself. Val.' She pauses for a breath and her large bosom rises with the effort, showing off the silver badge worn by the club president.

'I'm Roy,' he says, gaining from Val's friendly stewardship.

'Same as my uncle. Now he was a character, always tinkering. He built a ship in his front yard. Nobody thought it would ever get to the water's edge, but it went and flooded, didn't it, and nobody reckoned on that. Just goes to show, doesn't it? May says that fish can fly.' Val leads Roy down one level of steps to the S level, which is crowded with boutiques and homeware stores. They pass through automatic doors that open on to the street and there is the big blue and white P sign that first pulled Roy underground.

'Here you go then,' says Val.

Roy wants to embrace her. She waddles off, turning once to wave at him as he stands waiting under the shade of a shop awning. He badly needs to pee but dares not leave his post to search for a public toilet. Sweat has sodden his armpits and matted his grey hair. He studies a hairdressing salon window and sees the reflection of the road-service van cruising to a halt. Roy waves frantically at the driver, as if hailing a paramedic. He gets into the passenger seat, tension easing as he nears the end of his ordeal. Another saviour. This one is middle aged, with short sandy hair and a dark goatee.

'Locked the keys in the car, did we? Never mind, there's a first time for everything,' he says, generously diminishing Roy's liability. 'Now, which floor are we on?'

'Down,' says Roy, panic returning as he strains to remember where his car is parked. 'But I'm not sure which floor.'

'These floors don't have numbers, do they? They're colour coded, if I'm right.'

'It's orange,' says Roy, taking a punt as they pass through avenues of pink pillars. Orange is next. No sign of Roy's car. They descend into blue. Roy searches for landmarks and the man slows as he turns again.

'It must be the next one,' promises Roy, and as they round the sharp corner from the ramp, there is his car blocking their path, its engine purring. A small crowd greets their arrival with hoots and whistles. Roy clambers out, crunching the toddler's dummy under foot.

The service man winks at Roy. 'You're lucky to escape alive.'

Roy is too drained to reply. His heart lurches as he watches the man work to unlock the car. What about Beth? He has been gone almost two hours.

'There,' says the man, handing Roy his keys. 'You know something? My mum keeps a spare on a magnet stuck behind the bumper bar. Good insurance.' He nods and sends Roy a sympathetic smile. 'These things usually happen in threes.'

JANET ENTERS THE kitchen, her eyes skating from dirty dishes on the bench to the smudges on the wall where Harry has bounced a wet tennis ball. The cat is mewing at the back door to be let in and fed. Picked from the dregs of a litter at the RSPCA, she has the tabby markings of a shotgun pedigree and avoids human contact. Janet holds the door open with her foot and feels the mugginess muscle inside. The cat streaks past her and crouches under a low bench, waiting for the castanet rattle of dry food in her metal bowl.

There is a weekend languor to the morning. She bends to open the dishwasher and stow the wine glasses she and Nick took upstairs last night when a howling shape leaps out from behind the pantry door. She drops a glass and explodes at Harry, who's laughing at his bulls-eye.

'Look what you've done. Why do you always cause trouble?' She picks him up and removes him from the splinters of crystal. 'Now get away while I clean up. The last thing I want to do is to spend Saturday morning in Casualty.'

This is the chorus of their relationship. His impulsiveness, her overreaction. Each time he catches her off-guard, she lashes out with her tongue. He moves so quickly and instinctively. She moves just as fast, just as often, and sometimes they collide. She had never stopped long enough to regard herself and her moods until Harry came along. So used to being the lucky one of a sibling pair, she is now, slowly, coming to appreciate the way kinship threads are woven like the tartan of a highland clan. Variant patterns of intemperance colour her family. The crimson of Cassie bleeds into Janet's cloth, which Harry is cut from.

Squatting to sweep up the glass, she scoops up a yellow Post-it pad that Harry has filled with pen doodles. On each page he has drawn a face. Mr Cool Dude has a pierced ear. Mr George Smoke has narrow eyes and a cigarette in his mouth. Mr Big Nose Butthead has a gigantic trunk jutting from his brow. Blondie Sharp Nose has one that's pointy, like a teacher's pencil. Mr Different has one square eye and one round, one spiky eyebrow and one cocked upward in a contemptuous expression of 'so?'

There are days when she adores mothering Mr Different. And there are days when she can't admit to the thoughts that sometimes flicker through her head. Last week Harry had been invited to a birthday party, cause enough for celebration, but when she picked him up, he was barefoot, mud stained, frenetic and altercating with the Bevan boy, who ran to his mother complaining, 'Harry pushed me over and called me a bitch.' Mrs Bevan ticked her son off for dobbing. She's unimpeachable, as close to perfect, in public, as a mother can be. Janet secretly envies this family, even as she dubs them the Von Trapps, to the mirth of her colleagues, who also view the Mrs Bevans of this world with the scepticism they reserve for the vow to honour and obey. Mrs Bevan is musical, with a flair for interior design and four children who always look as though they have been dressed for an eisteddfod. They behave beautifully, too. So does their damn dog. All her life Janet has fallen short when measuring herself against others; those who are cleverer, more beautiful; those who are singled out for success. She cannot break the cycle of wishing Harry could be more like the rest. Less himself.

She thinks of the tapestry he wove around the legs of the dining room chairs, using balls of wool found in an old bag in the laundry. She'd photographed this soft sculpture, with its spray of pale shades and the bolder blue of a jumper she had started to knit but never finished, wishing that she could preserve his woollen doodle for ever. On the good days she feels blessed by Harry's gifts and uncanny powers of perception. Unnerved, too. The weather isn't all that he deciphers. He sees signs in faces that strike her as curiously blank. He can smell a far-off fire before smoke flavours the air. He can hear a spider spinning at night outside his window, before first light glitters the web. Her son reads tones of voice, cottoning on to the tensions between her and Nick that their words are meant to conceal.

The last page of Harry's Post-it pad makes her laugh. Mr Scaredy Cat. Terror is exaggerated in every feature, its mouth recoiling and the eyeballs rolling to see who is creeping up from behind. Anxiety personified.

'That kid's got balls,' she had heard one of the fathers say admiringly when Harry insisted on racing Angus, champion Nipper, at the school swimming carnival. 'Anything's possible, Mum,' Harry had told her that day. This is the same boy who curls up in a pod of trepidation. The very same one who eats up patience, forgiveness and empathy.

Dale thinks it would be wise to have Harry evaluated by a psychiatrist, if his teacher's concerns persist. Janet prays their son's problems might work their way out, like a splinter of wood from skin. She would rather believe in the rich variance of human nature than live with the idea that her child needs medication, or the uglier notion that she has contributed to his developmental wobbles through nature or nurture. She is all too aware that Nick's steadiness balances her flightiness.

Janet first spotted Nick on the daily ferry ride from Manly to Circular Quay. His slight build, wispy brown hair creeping over the collar of his suit and an almost melancholy countenance made him difficult to peg in the guessing game she played to pass the journey. She thought he must have been a broker, judging from his avid reading of financial newspapers. But on their third encounter he had his head in a medical textbook on the female reproductive system; it took Janet considerable craning in the peak-hour crush to decipher the title. When they were introduced formally at a wedding – he knew the bride, she had dated the groom; they were the only guests unattached – Janet asked what it was about fallopian tubes that fascinated him. She admitted to perving at him on the ferry but he feigned ignorance of the dark-haired woman who clambered onboard in a rush, clutching a takeaway coffee and flicking her cigarette butt into the boat's backwash. Strangely hurt, Janet had turned away, determined never to show interest in him again. Nick learnt over time that her emotions were mercurial. Her volatility excited him, while he was her first glimpse of solid ground.

She hears the plaintive cries of Mel. 'Mum! Harry's in my room.'

'Harry,' she calls out, 'go and get the newspaper.'

There is a moment of quiet and then she hears his manic giggle – the laughter sets her on edge – then the sound of him sprinting through the house and leaping off the steps, game as anything. He races back inside with dewy grass on the soles of his feet, thumping the rolled-up newspaper on every surface within reach. He rips the plastic off, shredding it onto the floor.

They have begun reading the weather together every morning. This is Dale's idea, so that Harry can understand atmospheric patterns and prepare for changes that most people register with nothing more complicated than disappointment or delight.

Janet puts the kettle on while Harry straightens the paper out on the floor, practically under her feet. '"A fine and partly cloudy day",' he begins chirpily, then pauses, his voice quietening as he reads further. '"Scattered showers and isolated thunderstorms to the west".' He stands and looks out the window at the grey sky. 'What's "isolated" mean?'

Janet pulls out a clump of teabags and sets one at the furthest end of the kitchen bench. 'There. That's isolated,' she says. 'Isolated means on its own, a long way from Harry.' She smiles, but gloom descends as he struggles with doubt over the notion of a thunderstorm confined.

He returns to the map and its icons. 'I wish we lived in Coober Pedy,' he says.

Janet laughs – it's the only place on the map that always scores a smiling sun with dark glasses. She squats beside him. 'It's so hot there that people live underground,' she explains. 'I don't know if you'd like it much.'

Nick enters, wearing runners, shorts and a singlet, his socks emblazoned with the same corporate logo that rides his chest. Usually he leaves for his daily seven-kilometre run before the family wakes, but in a concession to weekend slovenliness he's allowed himself the luxury of a half-hour sleep-in. Janet sometimes wishes she had his ability to cleave to a pattern, the same instinct that guides Mel.

'Harry wants to live in Coober Pedy,' she announces.

Nick grins at his son. 'You'd die of boredom. The Aboriginal people call it *arabana*, which means "white person's hole".'

Janet smirks, wondering where he plucked this opal of nonsense from. She stands up and kisses his neck and he returns with a hug that barely qualifies before setting his stopwatch and bounding out the front door.

Harry has ranked today's forecast and decided it is a 'white cloud day', which means 'room for improvement but otherwise okay'. He fills his breakfast bowl with cereal, letting the flakes spill over the top.

'Can I have someone over to play?' he pleads.

She dreads the weekend ring-around, wending her way through the classlist like a telemarketer, trying not to let the knockbacks sadden her spirit. Some Saturdays she stumbles across news of a party he has not been invited to, and she flinches at his exclusion. Thirty years ago, she watched Cassie go through a similar cycle of rejection.

He kneels on the floor, poring over the telephone numbers, then dials up his first invitation. The annoyance she sometimes feels at his neediness melts when she hears his cheerful voice deepen with disappointment.

She reaches for the self-raising flour, deciding to surprise him with pancakes. As he puts the phone back in its cradle, she can feel the cold, moist tingle preceding rain.

ROY RECLINES HIS chair to a near horizontal position and curls up. He has told Beth the sequence of events that led to Val rescuing him, but hasn't let on to how scared he'd felt at losing traction. Laid out like the exhibits in a court case, these events might point to nothing more than a bad day, or to deep structural cracks in his foundation. Everybody forgets things. He has always had an appalling memory for names, particularly, he is embarrassed to admit, polysyllabic foreign names. Beth usually saves him. Perhaps his dependency has wasted muscles that should have been exercised daily.

Everybody knows that age weakens your recall. Only last week he had read a letter to the newspaper from an 85-year-old man who said his best birthday present was that people now expected him to forget their name or face.

Beth quotes Mora's theory, that these little white-outs are a part of learning to slow down. Mental blanks, Mora says, happen to elders, just as children graze knees when they start to run harder at life. Beth herself has begun to keep notes, jotting reminders of things to do on the back of recycled envelopes. Perhaps he should do the same, and stick a spare key behind the bumper bar, like the road-service man suggested.

A chill seeps into his bones even as the sun burns through the clouds to warm his shed. He could not bear to disintegrate. To be discarded like a jigsaw with missing pieces. At least cancer can be beaten into remission. Dementia is crueller. How would Beth cope? With him yet without him?

When he arrived, an hour and a half late, to collect her from yesterday's Pilates class, she joked that she didn't need a ride home – after three strong coffees, she was going to jog beside the car. She had called the bluff of the dragon breathing fire in his head, making light of his misery. 'Next thing, you'll have to carry one of those plastic IDs on a string around your neck.'

This was how it always worked – she made him feel secure. She always had.

At home, she gave him a quiz that she said would sort out whether his memory was functioning. 'First question. Who was secretary of the Chatswood East tennis club in 1960?'

'Graham Volley,' he responded, laughing. It's a private joke, one of those absurdities that chronicle a shared past. The man's phone number had been painted on a sign outside the tennis club in the street where they had once lived. Neither of them played tennis but they made a game out of asking each other, 'Have you called Graham yet?' If the harried response was 'Graham who?', there would be a smile of victory.

'Second question. Which sculpture by Lazlo Moholy-Nagy does your wife admire?'

'I've never known why,' he said promptly. 'Do you remember the first time we visited Manhattan to see it? It was freezing and you bought a pair of boots.'

Beth smiled. How could she forget? Each new telling was embellished according to the audience and the mood of the narrator. Sometimes the story was told to evoke New York in the bitterest of winters, sometimes the joy of seeing in the flesh works of art they had known only in reproduction. Other times, it illustrated the contrast between Beth's occasional extravagance and his Calvinist restraint.

Their Manhattan shopping expedition was more vivid in her memory than the sculpture. There had been two pairs of boots to choose from. One pair, in green snakeskin with hand-tooled red stitching, a dainty heel and elegantly toed, was ordained for the catwalk. The other pair was built for endurance, in black leather with heavy soles. Beth hankered after the green snakeskin. They made her want to tango. Roy said it was a choice between Bauhaus function over les Folies Bergere froth. She bought the stout pair, immediately regretting her prudence.

On the subway back to their lodgings she had sat next to an elderly man who seemed ancient but was probably younger than they are now. He was humming to himself, a lullaby that Beth had last heard from the lips of her grandmother. She was straining to catch the words when Roy whistled to her from the doorway, announcing their stop. In the rush to get off, she forgot the boots, in a box at her feet.

Beth assumed that Roy reminded her of this incident to prove that memory plays tricks on all ages. He had been wonderful that day in New York, insisting they go back to the store for the snakeskin boots, which had waltzed out the door moments before they burst back in, panting from their run up the hill. Later that day he bought her a beautiful aquamarine cashmere scarf. She still has it in a box somewhere, saving it for those special outings. The best come unannounced, so the scarf has rarely been worn.

She listened to his account of the car-park mishap without betraying even a shadow of concern. She didn't want to rattle him, to tip out his troubles before they could be sorted.

She hated her deceit. He loathed his. She worried that his absent-mindedness was like the first spray of loose stones announcing a landslide. He heard their flinty chip down the cliff-face, too. He lay awake that night, ticking off names from the past, titles of artworks, exhibition dates, sifting through the midden of his life, afraid that this was the beginning of their managing the separation to come, afraid that distance would grow between them as they shouldered each unexpected turn.

Beth rings Stephanie as soon as Roy disappears into his studio. Steph had retired in Adelaide with her husband, who died two years ago of a stroke while they sat in a movie theatre. She thought he had just nodded off, as he always did, and waited until the credits began to roll before nudging him.

Steph has copped the lot – two miscarriages, adultery, and now widowhood. She scoffs at Beth's fear. 'You can't compare Roy to Aunty Connie. Didn't you say that he was just on some kind of seminar panel at the university?'

'I know. I've been telling myself the same thing,' Beth says doubtfully.

'Where's Roy now?'

'Out the back.'

'Working?'

'Yes. At least I think so.' Beth turns towards the studio, hoping for confirmation, but hears nothing.

'You'll be laughing about this come Christmas.'

'I guess you're right.'

'If you knew how unreliable I've become lately, you'd be worrying about me. Our family's the one with the leaky gene. Have I told you what happened with my pearls?' She barely pauses for an answer. 'Tell me if I've told you this story. I've told so many people I've lost track. Anyway, I was going to wear them to Di's eightieth.'

'Di? Di who?' Beth is beginning to feel dizzy. Is the world going mad or just her immediate family?

'You know who I mean. She used to live next door. The flagpole house and the funny husband?'

Beth vaguely remembers him for the bees he kept on the back verandah and the honey he offered to the children who came for sweets one Halloween. He'd won Beth's respect there. She abhors this American import, hates that its door-to-door quest for treats has intruded upon a calendar already choc-a-bloc with celebratory days, all involving the purchase of a gift or a badge or a twist of ribbon.

'The point is,' Steph continues, clearly enjoying her yarn, 'I couldn't find the pearls in my jewel box so I rang the children to see if I'd lent them out, but I hadn't. I was on the verge of reporting a burglary when I had this flash about a gumboot. Sure enough, there they were, inside the toe of my old gumboot in the garage. I'd put them there months ago when number eight was robbed. So there you have it.'

Beth loves the way her sister is a champion of what she calls one-down-manship. Steph always manages to dredge up a story about herself to make you feel better. As she prattles on, Beth feels her alarm dissipate, a little.

The call ends and Beth makes her way to the couch, slowly bringing each leg up to rest on the cushions. Her legs and hips ache. The air is moist. Rain on the way but so far nothing has fallen but scattered drops that you can count as they polka dot the dusty ground. Country towns cratered by years of drought are running out of water altogether. Giant cracks honeycomb the earth's baked crust. The soil in garden beds is powdery and water repellent.

She can't see inside Roy's studio, relying on the music of his movement to notate the composition taking shape, to signify that all is well. Today there is silence and the overcast sky mirrors her mood. In this instant before the whip crack of thunder, she braces for a change in the rhythm of their lives. They have both nursed a desire to die in the arms of sleep. Who doesn't? When Roy's former art teacher had gone soft with a stroke and talked nonsense in verse, there had been a scramble amongst their circle to draw up living wills, sanctioning friends to release them from such an unsavoury end.

Beth's mother died of a brain haemorrhage while standing on a ladder to fix the curtains, keeling over when the girls were at school. Steph had found her on the floor, in pleats of crushed red satin. Their father put the curtains in a box under the house. He installed blinds on the living-room window, and the blank screens offended the girls' memory of their mother's silky touch.

Sadness wells inside of Beth. She misses both her parents, still. She looks out at the stumpy frangipani tree and remembers her father remarking once on the melancholy of late afternoon. In the eaves outside the back door, wasps are building a nest high up, out of harm's way.

Keep moving, she tells herself.

'I'M FAMOUS,' SAYS Beth, handing a crumpled copy of the *North Sydney Times* to Billy, who has driven up from the south coast for his parents' forty-sixth wedding anniversary. His recent promotion to Director of Nursing at Lillipilli Aged Care Lodge provides a second excuse for partying.

'Even Tas says you were the talk of the bowls club,' grins Dale, pouring a glass of champagne for her brother. She takes a knife from its wooden sheath on the bench and chops a bunch of basil leaves with swift jabs.

'"Trendy cafe upsets patron",' Billy reads. He sips from his fluted glass, the nectar of family company warming him. A squat blue vase bearing Mora's thumbprint holds the pink sprigs of daphne he picked for Beth on his way to the front door. He scans the article, smiling.

A 74-year-old woman has vowed never to return to Paradiso, a Bay Rd cafe, after a waiter demanded, 'Who's in charge of this woman?' Beth Worboys of Kirribilli, who uses a walking frame, told the *Times*: 'No one was in charge of me. I was made to feel like a pet monkey, but I don't make a habit of wearing a collar and chain.' The proprietor, Amy Wilkes, strongly defended the waiter's concern, claiming that Mrs Worboys had looked unstable. Ms Wilkes also said that the waiter had been acting in the best interests of Mrs Worboys. 'It's a very fast, crowded place here and she could've hurt herself. The waiter assumed that somebody must be looking after her – a nurse or a relative.'

'Oh yeah,' Billy scoffs. 'He wasn't scared you might fall. He was terrified you might sue if you fell. It's not your broken bones he's worried about, it's legal costs.'

Dale joins in. 'Mum could sue them for presuming she might fall. Psychological injury, diminished respect. It's not the physical harm so much as the personal slight.'

Roy sits at the table, drawing his wife's profile with a thick red stub of pencil on a folded piece of butcher's paper. The children are used to their mother carrying the conversation while their father's hands polish or whittle or draw. They have always said that her mouth and tongue compensate for the stiffness of her body.

'Well, you've no idea the hoo-ha I've caused,' Beth boasts.

'Storm in a coffee cup.' Dale winks at Billy.

'Don't think I haven't cracked that joke myself a hundred times,' sniffs their mother.

'More like a cyclone,' quips Roy from the sidelines.

Beth laughs and hugs him with her eyes. 'A woman from the *Times* rang this morning to say the story's touched a raw nerve. She said the phone's been running hot with messages of support from people with axes to grind. One woman is taking the council to court because she can't manoeuvre her electric scooter past the sidewalk cafes to get to the shops. Who were the others, Roy?'

'The human can-opener?'

'Of course.' Beth slaps the table. 'A man who says he's broken his teeth trying to open tins of food.'

A shot of laughter draws the family together around the oak table.

'And then there was the woman who catches the bus and says no one stands up to give her their seat.' Beth is on a roll. 'Private school boys leave their sportsbags, laptop computers, tennis racquets and trumpets strewn across the aisle.'

'All the usual, run-of-the-mill human rights abuses,' says Roy, twinkling like his old self so that Beth wants to sing.

'Don't laugh,' Billy counters earnestly. 'Mum's on to something here. Neglect of elderly people is the next creature to come crawling out from under the rocks. An aged-care place up north was hauled into the coroner's court for starving people to death, literally. Residents on walking frames went begging for food from the houses nearby. And the Catholic nursing home where I worked last year, they used to schedule a bus trip when the government's accreditation team descended. It was the only organised activity all year. Management had been cutting corners on incontinence pads and night staff. One weekend a former POW was left on the toilet for four hours. He'd locked himself in and no one heard him screaming for help.'

An uneasy pause alerts Dale to a conversational deadend. She hands Billy the cutlery and points him towards the dining room. She follows him in with the dish of fish curry, its fragrance lifting their spirits.

On the wall is a large photograph of the four of them beachcombing in Murramurang National Park, walking off an easter lunch. Beth's mouth is open in mid-sentence and Roy's coat pockets bulge with treasures from the shore.

Next to the photo is a gift Roy made for Beth on her sixtieth birthday, a wooden curio box filled with rows of seedpods at different stages of ripeness. Beth loved it, but he'd apologised for his modest role in arranging nature's designs. The pods remind her of what she feels for him. Full to bursting with love.

Roy brings in the good china plates and, as Dale garnishes each serving with coriander leaves, Billy fills their glasses dangerously close to the brim. He pulls out his chair and there on the dark brown velvet is a white cardboard box.

'Pour moi?' He flourishes his find, grandly opening the lid, then closing it quickly as he looks from Beth to Roy.

'I'm afraid there's no reward for finding that,' Beth says breezily. 'It's Mora's. She bought a pie for lunch and then she lost it.'

'To my darling,' says Roy, raising his glass in a toast to her deft preservation of his dignity.

JANET KICKS OPEN the gate and lugs her suitcase up the steps. She has been in Cairns, covering the aftermath of a cyclone that drowned the northeast coast. Hanging up her coat, she frowns at the creep of mildew dusting the shoulder of Nick's black leather jacket. Nothing, she reminds herself, compared to the damage where she's come from. One of the survivors she interviewed had spent a whole night on top of the roof, swatting at snakes while the flood waters cleaned out her house, home videos of her children floating by. Janet was staggered by her resignation at the weather's undoing.

When she rang home last night, Nick told her that Harry had been asking repeatedly whether there would be flooding in Sydney and pulling his T-shirt over his head so that he looked like a turtle when bursts of drumming rain fell. She imagined him standing by the window, frightened of looking, yet comforted by the absence of what he could see in his mind's eye. Nothing ever lured him from this post but her pledge that he would be the first to learn of impending disaster. She's a weather presenter – of course she'll warn him if the city is doomed.

Harry had come on the phone full of news of the board game he was inventing with his father. Now that the storm had passed, he was cheerful. 'On the front it says: "Storm Warning. A game by Harry and Nick Swan that is sort of like 'Snakes and Ladders' and 'Cluedo'. See inside for rules." Mel thinks the name's dumb. What do you think?' he asked eagerly.

Making fun out of fear had been Dale's idea.

She'd heard Nick's laughter in the background and felt a surge of love for him, his cool, rational approach to life unpolluted by swirls of impulsivity.

'It's sort of like "Snakes and Ladders", Mum. But you slide down umbrellas, or if you land on a rainbow, you go up. You miss three turns if you get caught in a storm and you jump ahead two spaces if you —'

Janet broke in to his chatter to take a call on her mobile from Harvey's PA. 'Harry, my other phone's going. I'll play with you when I get home tomorrow night. I promise.'

Nick, waiting to talk again with a wife gone for the better part of a week, couldn't believe that she had hung up.

'She had to take a work call,' Harry said dully.

Nick tried her mobile, which went to voicemail. A thoroughly modern man, he had never questioned Janet's drive.

But he now wondered, when waking at night or waiting for the lights to turn green, whether Janet's absences had handicapped Harry. Abandonment was a clanger of a word, one that he would never drop in earshot of the sisterhood, amongst women who had cleansed their lexicon of the emotional entanglement of mothering, who had embraced the cooler, contractual obligations of caring. He thought of his mother's lot, of her shock at learning she was pregnant with him, in an age when only the truly unlucky got pregnant at forty-plus, a stone's throw from the empty nest she had been looking forward to, the chance to see through plans of her own. Nick couldn't imagine Janet accommodating such a family-planning disaster.

That night he dreamt she had come home, but instead of carrying her suitcase, she cradled a bundle in her arms.

MOST PEOPLE FEAR something: crowds, darkness, spiders, fire, heights, flying, sharks, public speaking, commitment, failure. The secret is to manage the vulnerability. Sedate the emotional angst.

Janet is afraid of the warming, though she would never admit as much to Harry. She's okay watching satellite feeds of giant breakers clawing chunks of cliff and coastline into the sea, but would never volunteer for frontline reports as the hurricane lands. She hasn't needed to get any closer to the action than sweeping in after the low pressure system has passed. But now Harvey is hungering for the 'actuality' of live crosses, predicting that tracking weather will become a popular obsession. Inside, she quakes at the assignments that might flow from his prophecy. But the scarier prospect of being let go, or blown off her professional pedestal, means she will do his bidding.

This afternoon she has an appointment with Harry's teacher, at Miss Dobbin's request. Harry's disruptiveness in class is the only item on the agenda. Janet sometimes thinks she's the one who needs the shrink, because of the guilt she carries for Harry's insecurity. If she hadn't gone to work when he was young, would he be square jawed and solid? Jenny Monk and the other mothers at work ride this same merry-go-round. Swapping stories of being pulled between home and work, they agonise over the latest research into child development. They strip bare for each other, pardoned by their togetherness for the decision each has made separately, to break their mother's mould. They live crowded lives, arranging then rearranging days, duties and children to account for all the many, unexpected elements of love.

No matter how many times the literature acquits them of foul play, Janet prosecutes herself. She walks across the playground, waving at the janitor as he pushes his broom across the basketball court. Harry is one of his 'specials', as he calls the children who worship him. Janet knows Harry uses his cupboard as a bolthole when he's in strife or scared.

'How's my trick?' he calls to her, the humidity soaking his blue shirt.

'Haven't you heard?'

'What's that?'

'He's going to live in Coober Pedy.'

'I won't be going to visit him,' he laughs.

Miss Dobbin is waiting for her in the classroom. She welcomes Janet with thin civilities that barely disguise her exasperation. 'I'm having a few problems with Harry.' She tempers her words with a smile. 'First thing in the morning he's okay, but then his concentration slips away.'

Janet tries to offer a solution. 'Perhaps if he sits on his own, near the blackboard?'

'Believe me, I've tried sitting him on his own. I've tried sitting him smack in front of my desk. I've tried incentive systems. I've tried warning systems. But I'm afraid Harry's so easily distracted that he can't focus on a thing.'

'But he loved making his boat, remember?' No sooner are the words out of Janet's mouth than she remembers Nick finishing off the sail and icy-pole stick oars, while Harry entertained himself by hacking into the leftover blocks of polystyrene.

'I know he did, and I try to give all my students as many hands-on activities as I can. But frankly, Harry has me over a barrel. If I don't let him do exactly as he pleases, the fidgeting starts. He pulls at his shoelaces. He drops his pencils and tears his eraser into tiny pieces. And the problems aren't only in the classroom. He has trouble in the playground with waiting his turn and sticking to the rules of a game. It's almost as if he can't control himself, and I'm sorry to say that I'm fresh out of innovation.' She sighs heavily, signalling that such a defeat is rare for a woman who sprouts ideas at the rate most people shed dead skin. 'Now, I hoped you might be able to give me some advice on what works for you.'

Janet grapples with her response. How can she tell Miss Dobbin, who sits pert with expectation, that what she does is buckle up and hang on tight and sometimes the ride ends in a head-on smash while other times she climbs out of the carriage dizzy with the thrill of being alive. Truth being, she doesn't have a ten-point plan. Truth being, she is like her son. Truth being that when she was at school, teachers didn't label high-octane children or suggest medicating them.

Janet knows there are limits to society's tolerance of extreme behaviour and she worries about what will happen to the larger characters, the troublemakers. The stirrers like her son.

What was it Nick's mother said the day Harry painted a fresco with lipstick on the dining room wall? 'You can always turn the volume down on a child with spirit but you can't make a firecracker out of wet cardboard.' Janet took heart from her applause. Her own mother had hung on to the words of the teacher who found Cassie a breath of fresh air. Miss Dobbin, however, is gagging on lungfuls of carbon monoxide.

'There's an excellent specialist that the school uses for guidance in these situations and I think you should consider taking Harry for a consultation.'

Janet decodes Miss Dobbin faster than the teacher can sugar her message. She concentrates intensely on counting the freckles that dot her face, to ward off the final humiliation of a wobbling chin. She has stopped listening. Her sole mission is to get out of the classroom without tears. She thanks Miss Dobbin at twenty-five freckles and says she will talk it over with Nick. Outside the door, possibly eavesdropping, stands a breeder of scholarship candidates, children reared on piano lessons, flashcards and the grim ambitions of a mother's self-sacrifice. The woman is probably here to find out why her child only got nineteen out of twenty for maths. Janet nods a greeting and retreats to her car, where she sobs.

She rings Nick but his phone diverts so she tries his mobile and leaves a tearful message. She wipes her eyes and her nose with an old serviette she finds in her bag, wishing she had tissues in the glovebox instead of dead batteries and three quarters of a street directory. The car's interior is a mess – newspapers, press releases, video tapes, sunglasses minus a lens, one sock, a school excursion form and Harry's lollypop sticks litter the floor like cigarette butts. She rings Jenny Monk but the curt 'Yes?' of her answer says 'no time to talk'. Deadlines are like that. Nick has never forgiven her for staying at work to finish a story the day his father died.

She recovers enough to ring Dale and check on the paediatric psychiatrist Miss Dobbin is recommending.

'Simon Calvert specialises in neurological disorders. He's written a book on Attention Deficit Hyperactivity Disorder and he's highly regarded.'

'But what do you think of him?' Janet asks, keeping her breath steady.

'He's a psychiatrist, I'm a psychologist. We come at this from different disciplines,' Dale says. 'You and Nick have to talk about this.'

'Do you think Harry has a disorder?'

'I don't know, but school is often the place where serious problems become apparent. The teacher's only doing her job, okay? She's not the enemy.'

But how can Janet think of Miss Dobbin any other way? She starts the car and the windscreen mists with the finest sprinkling of rain. Her sunglasses darken the moth-grey sky but she needs them to mask her eyes.

COFFEE WITH DALE is cancelled, because of the rain. Roy once promised to attach an umbrella to Cuz, but Beth could see him then finding room for other accessories and reckoned that she would soon resemble a bag lady on wheels.

He heads for the studio after a breakfast of muesli and tea, unsure about the hot colours and cartoon images filling his sketchbook, which he forgetfully leaves on the kitchen table. She contains the urge to peek at the pages. She's always called his sculptures 'whatnots' when they're in gestation, foetal smudges on the ultrasound of his vision.

Puddles of water collect in the dips and troughs of the yard. Beth reads the newspaper at the kitchen table with an ear to the radio. The traffic is chaotic and the announcer alerts commuters to accidents at intersections, lights, freeway exits. A northbound tunnel is blocked by a truck wedged in the entrance, backing up cars for miles. Beth smiles smugly. Immobility has its upside.

Outside, the springy boughs of the bottlebrush are laden with the weight of the water that has been falling all night. The air clings like a woollen jumper. There is a photograph in the newspaper of a woman hoisting up her brightly patterned dress as water sloshes around her knees on a submerged traffic island in Marseilles. She holds her high-heeled shoes aloft in one hand. On the radio a meteorologist is being interviewed about Sydney's rainfall. Beth can't remember such a soaking. At her age, memories cluster around the big events – droughts and cyclones – just as births, marriages and grief steeple the horizon line of a life.

The radio announcer is warming to the weather as a topic that can take her right through to the news. The doorbell rings, but by the time Beth reaches the end of the hallway's Persian runner, the courier has sped off, leaving a damp package on the doorstep, an envelope from the *Times* with a bundle of mail and phone messages tucked inside, prompted by the front-page account of her outburst last week. She parks Cuz by the table and lowers herself into a hard-backed chair. The first envelope she opens is violet and addressed in a spidery hand. The notepaper has a floral border.

Dear Mrs Worboys

Three cheers for your brave stand. My son put me in Morningside Aged Care Hostel two years ago. I am in a wheelchair and a stroke has interfered with my ability to speak. I can write, but with some difficulty, as you can see. Six months ago he told me he was going to Algiers to work. He sent me a Christmas card but he has not answered my letters. The nurses are stretched to the limit and I do not like to trouble them. I have written letters to the newspapers, and the ministers for aging, federal and state, but no one takes the slightest notice. I am an optimist at heart and thought you sounded quite decent. Do you know anyone who could rescue me?

  Sincerely yours

  Ellen Diamond

If Beth was twenty years younger, she would rush to dust the spare room. But on second reading she discerns something else. Does Ellen want a one-way ticket out?

Nursing homes are holding pens; camps for refugees banished from the sovereignty of youth. How can anyone expect a few knickknacks to convince a person that this is where they belong? Some people get attached to institutions. Beth's uncle had lived in a home for the blind. He'd been packed off, with an old brown suitcase and framed photographs of his nearest kin, to a large gothic building with acres of linoleum and peeling green paint. Next thing, he refused family invitations for Sunday roast and before long he wouldn't even come for Christmas. He said they needed him to fold the sheets. The precision of putting corner to corner, with a tug to get the creases out, bound him to that place, marking the difference between a home and a transit lounge.

Beth will write to Ellen Diamond. Perhaps a letter will make her feel that she has been heard. As for the discreet reference to assisted suicide, this is a topic Beth has long mused on.

At the onset of arthritis, those long days weighed down by pain, she used to plan her funeral, a ghoulish game to part the gloom. There would be bouts of wallowing as she considered her choice of funeral music, the loudspeaker that the church would use to broadcast the service to the unexpectedly large crowd of mourners gathered outside.

She opens an official-looking envelope – an invitation to join Pensioners Alliance. Straight into the bin. She picks out a handwritten cream envelope from a mother she'd befriended when their sons were in Scouts together; the woman's boy has married and moved to Broome. Beth is hungry for more detail, always curious to see how children turn out. She is engrossed in her mail and does not notice Roy dripping at the back door.

'Tea?' he asks, rubbing his hands together. He wipes them on jeans streaked with paint and gobs of resin. The rain is heavier than it was and Beth hears the drip in the laundry roof that will need a bucket. Roy takes off his runners without undoing the laces and slips on his leather scuffs.

'Your shoes are on the wrong feet,' Beth says.

Roy looks at her, then at the shoes. 'The shoes aren't the problem. It's the feet.' His daffy expression leaves her none the wiser as to whether his remark is in jest.

She watches him opening and closing kitchen cupboards in a twitter; his thoughts are off elsewhere. He takes two black cups from the cupboard. She does not mention the two clean cups already out on the bench.

'How's it going in the shed?' she asks.

'The rain's got me going, given me a few ideas. I've decided to use water. Or the absence of water. A puddle, a large round puddle that used to be a dam.'

From these few clues, Beth hazards a guess. '"Water Restrictions"?'

'What?'

'Is that your working title?'

'No,' he laughs. '"Hot Water".'

'Try the kettle,' she says.

He laughs again. 'No, silly, that's my working title.' He bends and kisses her on the neck and she ripples with pleasure at the brush of his lips. He straightens up to look for the lighter to ignite the stove. 'Where's the thingamajig?'

'On its hook.'

His absorption pleases her. This is how he should be, gripped by the possibilities of conception.

He sits beside her at the table and picks up Ellen Diamond's letter. 'Diamond. Wasn't there a Diamond boy who used to play football with Billy?'

'Not that I remember,' she says, thinking through the faces on the sidelines of weekly sport fixtures.

Roy shrugs and presses his teabag against the rim of his cup, tanning the water. He opens the newspaper and scans the pages. 'There's been another break on the Ross Ice Shelf,' he reports, transfixed by the details.

Beth goes back to her letters and picks out a new envelope. Written in the pin-striped formality of fountain pen, this missive is from a Dr Robert Kinane, a naturopath and physician whose name she vaguely recognises.

I always like to acknowledge a fellow stirrer and one of my colleagues emailed me a report of your duel at the cafe. If you are interested, come and hear me speak. The Royal Australian College of Surgeons is hosting a symposium on death and dying next month.

Beth puts the letter aside, thoughtful. Just as scientists monitor the Ross Ice Shelf, she is measuring Roy's presence of mind. Perhaps she will contact this Kinane. What's the harm in making a connection?

She'll write after their trip. They are driving to Canberra

on Friday, for Roy's meeting with the architects in charge of the meteorological bureau project, and they'll be staying with Mora.

On the phone last night Mora had objected to Roy's use of the word enormity. 'Roy Worboys,' she chastised. '"Enormity" does not describe hugeness. You of all people! Heinous wickedness.'

'You're overstating the crime,' he scoffed.

'No, that's what enormity means,' she said with satisfaction.

He put the receiver down on the hall table, after promising to scuttle her in the compulsory game of Scrabble they will play on Saturday evening. He meant to tell Beth that Mora was waiting to speak to her, but forgot. Mora hung on for a good ten minutes, hollering occasionally into the receiver, but was answered only by the sound of shuffling feet.

TODAY HARRY IS pulled taut. 'There's nothing good to eat,' he says, swinging the cupboard door on its hinges until Janet is sure it will break. He wants Coco Pops. She should focus on the wars, not the skirmishes, but sugar and food colouring are linked to hyperactivity. These are the suburban terrorists, along with electricity towers, salt, mobile phones, gluten, childhood inoculations, video games, aluminium saucepans and mercury in fish. Janet cannot keep track of the studies pointing to poisons that were passed off yesterday as harmless.

Harry rips open the new box of cornflakes she finds and fills his bowl in a rush. As usual, the cereal overflows on to the floor, crunching under feet rarely still. Today she takes him to see Dr Calvert. She's full of misgivings and a night short on sleep has made her scratchier still.

After dinner Nick had set to filling out the form from Simon Calvert's office, ticking boxes, contorting truths about their son. They had to indicate the frequency of behaviour on a sliding scale from 'hardly ever' to 'very often'. But how often is too often, Janet wanted to know.

'"Does your child lose things?"' she read from the list.

'Yes,' said Nick.

'Only sometimes.'

'You spend half your life ferreting through the lost property bin at school. That's definitely a yes.'

'I'll put down "often".'

'Put "very often". There's no point going through this if you're determined to skew the results,' Nick said tersely.

'"Is your child always on the go?"'

'Yes.' They nodded and laughed.

'But he's a boy,' Janet protested. 'And what's wrong with being a goer? I'm on the go. That's what we say all the time about people: "he's got no get up and go". Go is good.'

'But you have to go in a constructive way. You have to go for something and finish the task. Not just bounce from one thing to another.'

Janet flushed. 'Isn't that what I do?'

His pause discredits the denial that follows. 'This is not about you. I simply said that Harry needs to harness his energy.' Nick's voice is low but she can tell he's a little annoyed.

'Maybe we've got him in the wrong school.'

'Maybe we have. But remember what the teachers said about him at kindergarten?'

'Why trust their judgment?'

'All I'm saying is that we could change schools and still find ourselves back on the couch filling out these forms again.' He pulled their conversation back to the questionnaire. '"Does your child avoid tasks that require sustained mental effort?"'

'Okay, so he's not going to be a brain surgeon. But look at Harvey, my boss. He left school at sixteen and he's done everything he set out to do.'

Nick cuts her off. 'Times have changed, Janet. You're such a romantic sometimes.' He ticks off the next item. '"Is your child often forgetful in daily activities?"'

Often, thinks Janet, who knows that she would score no higher than her son on these questions. She pours herself another glass of red. 'I'd like to try that physician I read about, the one who uses a Chinese herbalist and dietician to treat behavioural problems. What do you think?'

'Next you'll be hanging crystals above his bed.'

'I don't want to dope him up, Nick. I like him the way he is.'

'No, you don't. You're always at him. He's too frenetic, he's too demanding, he's difficult. "He's exhausting." That's your refrain.'

Janet lashed out. Not hard, but a punch thrown in fury at the home truth he had lobbed her way. If he had swung the blow, any jury would hang him for domestic violence; he'd be manacled.

She immediately regretted losing control. Nick seethed beside her, his breathing heavy with the effort of holding off from retaliation.

'This is poisoning us,' he said, low and deliberate, then removed himself upstairs.

Sloshing the last of the wine into her glass, she grabbed a light cotton quilt from the cupboard and settled on the couch. She hated him right now; hated his certitude. She chewed on her anger until the alcohol worked its trick, but she slept fitfully.

A garbage truck braking in the street opened her eyes before first light. She flew down the front steps, swinging the wheelie bin out the gate as the driver activated his metal claw. Wide awake, she pulled on canvas sneakers and headed towards the harbour's shore as day broke.

High tide had encrusted the water with plastic bags, empty Coke bottles and floating lilypads of trash. She felt like scum herself, wasted, adrift. A black dog plunged straight into the sea, paddling energetically to retrieve a tennis ball thrown into the drink. Back on land the dog put down his ball and shook to dry himself, spraying Janet's bare legs with cold salty drops.

She tells Harry about the dog as he ties his shoelaces tight, as if securing a corset; every few weeks they snap with his determined pull. He likes his shoes tight. He likes his underpants loose. He likes his socks halfway up his calf. Finicky, precise, black, white. His dislikes offer no slack for good-natured accommodation of the unforeseen.

They arrive at Dr Calvert's consulting suite ten minutes early. The lift shudders and Janet can see the fear in Harry's wide eyes at the possibility of being stranded in a windowless metal box, metres above ground.

In the waiting room Harry finds a *Where's Wally?* games book in amongst the tattered *National Geographic*s, but somebody has beaten him to it, circling the Wally on every page in black biro. Dr Calvert's patients arrive in pairs, two by two, mothers and sons. When Harry is called in for the first round of tests, Janet phones her office. Harvey is on the rampage – there's a cyclone careering towards the northwest coast. Towns are being evacuated, people fleeing any way they can.

But Janet is submerged in her own drama. Dr Calvert's book on Attention Deficit Hyperactivity Disorder is for sale on the counter and she flicks through the chapters, not wanting to read her son between the lines. Instead, she studies the boys in the waiting room. They all look perfectly normal; perhaps they are sedated already. Janet hears her name called. Dr Calvert is tall and skinny with steel-rimmed glasses and his office is bare of biographical lint. The framed prints could have been provided by the firm that waters the potted plants.

Harry is ushered in by the assistant who has completed an assessment of his literacy and concentration skills. His eyes light up at the sight of a swivel chair: a big, fat, ergonomically designed trap that he immediately sets in motion. Janet watches him spin. He ignores the questions Dr Calvert patiently puts to him; he's impervious to the bearing they will have on his future. For all Janet's dissembling on her tolerance of a decibel level that Miss Dobbin finds disturbing, Dr Calvert decides that Harry does suffer ADHD, in a mild form. Drugs are not prescribed. Held in abeyance. Kept in reserve.

Happy in the moment, however temporary, Janet floats out of his office, victorious at bringing Miss Dobbin to heel. Harry refuses to catch the lift again so they take the stairs. He bounds down two or three at a time, until the last turn when he rides the banister, no hands, right to the exit. She buys him a chocolate éclair that he eats in the car, smearing cream over the upholstery.

'Dr Calvert looks like a mad scientist,' he says, and Janet laughs. 'Do I have to go to school now?'

'Absolutely.'

'But it's swimming lessons today.' He hates the grind of answering instructions and stiffens in revolt. 'I'm not going.'

He rams his feet into the glovebox in rage and Janet smacks her hand down, catching her wrist on the handbrake.

'Stop wrecking the car.' She lowers her voice to keep the

illusion of control. 'You're always wrecking everything.' She thinks of the wooden panels on the door to his bedroom, cracked from furious slamming, and the car seats that have been attacked by hammering feet. 'I'm sick of your behaviour,' she says. 'I am sick of you getting into trouble at school.'

'Shut up!'

Harry screams so loudly that Janet crosses over to enemy lines. She is on the side of the teachers now. She is ready to surrender him. Mr Different is on his own. Mr Scaredy Cat can die of fright. They drive in silence. Janet's wrist smarts from colliding with the brake.

'When I have a kid I hope I don't have one like me,' he whispers.

Janet is demolished.

WINTER HAS BEATEN them to Canberra, disrobing the poplars that stand sentry around Lake George. Roy has always liked the national capital for its sharp seasons, for the cherry blossoms in spring and the dry intensity of summer's heat, when strips of eucalypt bark peel off and shed their skin. In autumn the liquidambars and claret ash preen then moult as public servants rug up in fleece and scarves. Mora reckons the cold is in retreat because the water pipes in her old government cottage no longer freeze in the early morning frost. Roy and Beth have brought along warm coats. Sydney's temperate climate has spoilt them and neither wears much padding on the thighs these days.

Mora is gardening when they turn into her pebbled driveway. She wipes loose dirt from her hands on a denim apron before hugging her guests, flicking a dangle of weed from Roy's jumper with a black-rimmed fingernail. She doesn't bother with tools and gloves, preferring to knead the earth like a ball of clay. Her garden is envied year round. Every summer, cars slow as people crane to see the spectacle of sweetpea that she trains into a beehive hair-do, smack in the middle of her front lawn. Roy calls it the tea-cosy.

Mora loves native plants but has no desire to imprison them in garden beds. She fields suggestions that she plant wattle and bottlebrush, to save water, by smugly claiming credit as the first in her suburb to install a rainwater tank under the eaves. The back garden has a lemon tree, two apple trees, a vegetable plot and herbs. Beth loves the bounty of Mora's place; somehow the spadework and weeding and growing that goes on here is a balm for her own stiffness. In the pantry, jars of preserved fruit and chutneys stand to attention in columns of burnt orange and red. Mora dispenses them generously and sells a few to restaurants, for decoration and the ripening of harvest they lend to a menu.

The death of her husband, Bob, has made little impression on the lively mess of Mora's habitat; he was always a bit player here, on parole from the Department of Treasury. Pensioned off ten years ago, he annexed a patch of her territory, building a small hothouse where he grew orchids, twenty-seven varieties, with the same bookish precision he had once applied to the nation's accounts. Mora's grief was just as efficient. The worst moment in the months following Bob's massive heart attack was her awakening to the ghastly admission that she did not miss him. She packed up his papers in boxes and took them to the tip. She gave his clothes to the Brotherhood: twenty-five ties, thin, fat, striped and spotted, and two charcoal suits. She didn't set out to kill the orchids but they pined for him. She rewrote her will and held a mammoth garage sale, spurring the neighbours to springclean their own cupboards and raising enough money to build a skateboard ramp for the reserve at the end of the street. Her kiln, stone cold from years of neglect, was donated to a community arts centre. Canberra rules the nation but runs like a country town.

Roy brings their bags inside and afternoon tea drifts into supper with a spread of cheese, sundried tomatoes and fresh bread, which they dunk into steaming bowls of potato and leek soup. The three begin as they usually do, catching up on mutual friends, sorting through names and faces as if foraging through a tin of antique buttons, discarding the dull ones and turning over in their hands the loudest and gaudiest. Mora is miffed by the resurrection of Laura Vallent, an artist who committed suicide forty-five years ago, after her female lover returned to the marital nest. Vallent had left behind tea-chests full of textile designs that have only just been rediscovered, by a fine arts graduate who'd been poking around bric-a-brac shops in the Blue Mountains. Soon there will be an exhibition of Vallent's work, followed by all manner of commercial spin-offs, Mora suspects. She donated a set of Vallent curtains that had been mothballed in her closet, waiting on their designer's posthumous acclaim. There's no doubting that the pattern of teacups silhouetted in black and set against splashes of coffee-bean dye is striking, but Mora holds to the belief that her own work is no less deserving of a second look.

Mora had been a potter, until four children and a husband ate into the space she had once stubbornly set aside for herself. When she shared a studio with Roy, some forty years ago, she had the shoulders of a swimmer and strong forearms from years of kneading clay into platters, teapots, bowls and pudgy candlesticks. But her career petered out as the demands of family grew and patronage dried up. Customers who had once loved the roughness of her goods now bought stainless steel and glass. She could have reinvented her wares in bright colours and smooth surfaces but concentrated instead on teaching her craft to pensioners. Some days she blames motherhood for burying her creative streak. Other times she snorts at this excuse. Either way, she refuses to see herself as a victim.

Roy is one of the few colleagues who continues to regard her as a serious talent. This counts. He believes in her work, and regarded her as a fellow crusader when the cringe sidelined Australian art.

Mora dispenses with Vallent to mull over the fate of a painter who has become addicted to cough medicine, the bottles in his coat pockets clinking like a musical score. 'He always liked a drink,' she says. 'Remember in Broken Hill when he came back from the pub and collapsed and you had to take his class?'

Roy has absolutely no idea what she is talking about. 'When was this?' He looks to Beth, who's usually ready to prompt him, but she's shuffling out of the room.

Mora is astonished. 'Broken Hill, nineteen sixty-two. I don't believe you could wipe that out,' she says, in humorous reproach. 'We were there for seven months.'

'Of course.' He smiles, as he is learning to do, but the camouflage does not trick Mora and for a moment she is the one caught off balance, embarrassed for having tripped him up.

Their awkwardness is salvaged by her Burmese cat, Sumi, almost expiring at Roy's feet. Stricken with bowel cancer, blind, deaf and incontinent into the bargain, she staggers drunkenly from the deathbed Mora has constructed by the fireplace out of an old washing basket and faded pink silk kimono. Roy picks her up and strokes her on his lap, retreating from Broken Hill as fast as he can, to the safer territory of Sumi's unpromising future. But as Mora takes him through the pros and cons of having the cat put down, he can hear the disquiet in her voice. He can see that her eyes regard him differently.

Roy wants to confide in Mora. She knows him so thoroughly. But he rebuffs the desire to tell all, just as once, long ago, he had resisted the desire to seduce her, wary of doing anything that might destroy their friendship. Instead, he keeps stroking the cat, grateful for her warmth on his knee. They exhaust the subject of the cat, including the therapeutic role of pets for the elderly, sick and lonely.

'What a winning trifecta,' says Beth, laughing as she rejoins them in the sitting room, which is cluttered and comfortable with its club lounge and walls of books, their spines creased, pages sprouting strips of paper to mark reference points. The shelf closest to Mora's chair is full of dictionaries – classical, literary, biographical and one dedicated to quotations. Underneath are books fat with art reproductions and a tattered but complete set of the *Australian Journal of Pottery and Ceramics.*

'Who's up for Scrabble?' Mora bullies.

'You promised we could have twenty-four hours' breather,' Beth says. 'I've got car lag and you know very well, Mora Wallace, how you hate to win in a walkover.'

'I'm rusty,' Mora says slyly. 'My regular punching bag's sulking.'

'Not Martin?'

'Pathetic, isn't it. He says he's too tired since he began volunteer guidework at the National Gallery. I tell him there's no use hiding behind the cloak of public service, but I suspect a love interest in there somewhere.'

Roy is grateful for the easy chatter of Mora and Beth, who drift into the terrain of family and Beth's unrequited desire for grandchildren. Mora has five, with a sixth on the way. She chooses to be called Grand Mora rather than Grandma, to stand out from the flock of cream cardigans that sweep into the primary school playground for Special Person's day.

Beth is jealous. Listening to Mora's stories, she can't help hoping that her own children will extend the family. Mora revels in her matriarchy even as she scorns the crown and assorted duties this office bestows. She refuses to perform regular babysitting. Her own parents were never on call and what was then a source of constant frustration now serves as useful precedent, freeing her up for bridge, which she plays competitively with a tightknit group.

Mora rises from her chair and leaves the room to fetch a photograph of seven-year-old Phoebe, granddaughter number three. 'My favourite. Sacrilege, I know, to pick one out, but we all do, don't we? Billy was yours, wasn't he, Beth?'

'He was least like me, if that's what you mean. Sensitive, more vulnerable. Dale has my resilience, though now I wonder if I pushed her too hard. I wanted her to achieve in a way that I hadn't, and she's done that. She has her own practice. She speaks at schools and conferences around the country. But she's lonely.'

'She has her cats,' Roy says. 'And company doesn't necessarily cure loneliness.'

He lifts Sumi from his lap gingerly, as if carrying a Ming

vase, and deposits her in the basket. He bends to kiss them both good night, excusing himself on the pretext of preparing for tomorrow's meeting.

'The sculpture,' Mora says, guilty. 'We haven't touched on it.'

'Tomorrow,' he yawns.

She makes a mental note. Tomorrow: Scrabble. Sculpture.

On his bed Roy finds a scrapbook left open at a page with a newspaper clipping. 'Sculptor Extracts Awe' says the headline, above a story about an art train that visited Broken Hill as part of an adult education program to teach arts and craft to miners and their wives. The small black and white photograph is of a young man in shirt sleeves. Handsome and raffish, his eyes are bright with anticipation. He holds a cigarette between the elegant fingers of his right hand and chalk in the other. 'Sydney sculptor Roy Worboys draws a crowd to class' says the caption. There is a date in a corner: Monday 27 June 1962.

Roy scans the picture and words but he cannot retrieve this episode. Images, faces, smells, landscape – all proof of that journey is missing from his archives.

A CAMERA CREW is camped outside the Commonwealth Bureau of Meteorology as Roy backs into a parking space. Sipping coffee from takeaway cups, they case his arrival but are underwhelmed by his diffident bearing and make no move to film him. Old man, they think uncharitably, and resume their assessment of a trainee sound technician's sexual preferences.

Phillip Bennett rang Roy this morning to warn him that their meeting might be disrupted. The prime minister is resisting international pressure to curtail the warming and the media is staking out Bennett in the hope of filming the rant he usually delivers off the record – to protect his superannuated position, some critics say. Bennett is a suit-and-tie greenie. He did not march with the muddy foot soldiers on the banks of the Franklin or chain himself to the massive trunks of old-growth trees. Not for lack of passion. The son of a trade union leader who won every battle but lost the war, he chose not to abandon the comfort zone of polished teak negotiating tables, where intergovernmental committees wrestle over commas and clauses to the tinkle of teacups against gold-rimmed saucers.

The bureaucrat met Roy for the first time five years ago, when his wife, Sandra, commissioned Roy to make a garden sculpture for her husband's fiftieth birthday. 'Gone Bush' was the result. Roy made casts from Bennett's old leather hiking boots and stamped bronze footprints into the grass leading towards an arc of beaten metal. The feet continue up the arc, cut out around the soles to create small windows, silhouetting a path heaven bound.

Before the commission Bennett and Roy had been vaguely aware of each other as fringe dwellers in the environmental movement. Although separated by several decades, they both hunt the weather's sinister extremes. Grim statistics and dire predictions, however unwelcome, are traded between them, to bolster their pessimistic resolve in the face of stragglers who insist that natural variability explains the earth's warming.

Bennett's contract expires at year's end. He has fast-forwarded plans to build new headquarters for the bureau, so that he can leave his imprint on the landscape of public policy, even as his advocacy in the corridors and meeting rooms of Canberra loses its clout.

Roy approaches double glass doors that slide open, his stomach tightening in an allergic reaction to offices and fluorescent lights. Institutions swamp him with the sickly smell of compromise. He is jumpy, too, at what is happening inside his head – paths he could once walk blindfolded now leave him groping for guidance. Social engagements, always onerous, carry new risks. He is nervous of stumbling like he did last night, and the week before last, each instance blistering soft skin.

Inside the foyer is a reception desk with no one in attendance. Clutching his satchel, Roy checks his watch then examines a display of satellite images until a sullen-looking secretary arrives to escort him through the linoleum corridors, her platform shoes skewing as she draws him in her wake. She shows him into a timber-panelled lobby where two labourers are fussing over the height to hang a large photograph of a freak wave exploding over a stone boardwalk. Three matchstick figures cling to a spindly railing, trousers and jackets billowing in the wind. A fourth person has turned to make a dash for safer ground, beyond the camera's frame.

Roy wishes for an epilogue and one of the workmen reads his mind. 'Amazing that only one of them died,' he says. Roy knows instinctively which of the four was swept away.

Bennett sits at his computer in an office overlooking the Brindabella mountain range. Canberra has none of the shout and sparkle of Sydney's harbour, or its metropolitan scruff, but there is a sense of proportion to the artificial lakes, tree-lined avenues, roundabouts and memorials. The bush is boss, for all the spick and span of officialdom.

Bennett rises from his desk and greets Roy with a firm handshake. 'Thanks for coming down.'

'I can see you're not going quietly,' Roy replies, gesturing out the window at the camera crew.

'They're waiting for me to shoot my mouth off, and eventually I will. The prime minister believes that the warming is a conspiracy theory, end of story, so the sooner I go, the better. It's giving me cancer. Anyway, how have you been?'

'Fine,' says Roy. 'I've been working in the studio and I think I'm going somewhere I've never been before.'

Bennett is delighted. 'Good. The bureau is in the mood for adventure.'

A secretary pops her head around the door to announce that Joanne Lobel and her sister-in-law, Martha, partners in the architectural firm of Lobel and Lobel, have arrived to discuss the progress of Roy's sculpture. Both women are middle aged and Roy recognises a kindred spirit in Joanne's dishevelled hair and loose-fitting slacks, but can guess that her informality is deceptive. A thirty-six million dollar project dictates orthodoxy.

Martha unscrolls plans from a long black tube and flattens them out for inspection. Roy had entertained a vision of a cupola sheltering the new building, in the shape of an umbrella, but the constraints of the taxpayers' purse have delivered plans for yet another bunker. The forecourt will be paved in marbled concrete tiles that won't be laid until his sculpture is bedded down. He's curious to extract details of wind tunnelling and how the elements will affect his work, but Bennett is bored.

'Show me again where my successor will sit. We need a plaque outside the door, "torture chamber".'

'We did toy with putting all the senior management in the basement,' Joanna laughs. 'The lower down the pecking order you get, the more panoramic your view and the bigger your office.'

The joking relaxes them.

'That's where you'll go,' Martha says to Roy, pointing to a cross on the plans that marks where his sculpture will sit.

'In the front yard,' he notes.

'A version of the garden gnome,' Joanna suggests, and her smile fades when Roy nods vigorously.

'What I'm planning to create could be as colourful as a gnome, actually.'

'That sounds like quite a departure from your past work,' Joanna says, nervously.

Roy shrugs. 'So I've changed.'

Joanna fiddles with her strand of resin beads and looks across at Martha in a private semaphore: 'here's trouble'.

Bennett, however, is intrigued. 'I told you Worboys would upstage the two of you,' he teases.

The Lobels laugh. Joanna too loudly.

Martha brings the meeting to order. 'We need to know what materials you'll be using, and the dimensions. Architects and sculptors can't work in isolation. They used to, and you've only got to look around Canberra to see some spectacular failures of collaboration.'

Bennett's secretary enters and hands him a message, which he scans before excusing himself. 'I'm going to have to leave you to this. The Opposition's got hold of a letter I wrote begging ministers to think of their grandchildren's future and the prime minister's courtiers are waiting.'

Roy applauds. 'Take a fire extinguisher.'

'Too late for that,' Bennett notes dryly. 'They're out for blood – mine. I'm better off with a drum of kerosene.'

Martha rolls up the plans and smiles at Roy. 'Tell us about your garden gnome.'

'I'm using industrial glass. Here, I'll show you a few drawings.' Roy reaches for his satchel. Inside is the scrapbook Mora left on his bed last night, his wallet, car keys and the slender white bones from a bird's skeleton, which he found this morning in the garden. He tries to keep talking as he feels around the seams of the bag, searching for the envelope of drawings he was sure he had packed. But he's forgotten it. Suddenly his tongue cannot scrape enough saliva to swallow and his heart races with panic.

Joanna's sympathetic. Diabetic, insulin slump, mini stroke, senior citizen's moment? she wonders. This show of frailty is at odds with the man's reputation for robustness, for sculptures that endure extremes of wind, rain and heat.

'I have brought drawings . . . at least I thought I had . . . but they aren't where I'm sure I put them this morning. Do you mind waiting while I check and see if they're in the car?'

Martha glances at her watch and thinks, Be quick, as she smiles and tells him to go right ahead.

'I don't know what's got into me,' Roy explains feebly. He makes for the door, feeling as insignificant as the man in the photograph who ran from the wave.

Joanna flicks through a magazine, pausing at an article about flowers blooming out of season, because of the warming. Her crepe myrtle's scarlet splash was weeks premature.

Martha downloads emails from her BlackBerry, voicing impatience at Roy's absence. The artist had been thrust upon them by Phillip Bennett. She had suggested ten younger candidates, up-and-comers whose work she admired, who would bring an edge of controversy to the project, but Bennett would not budge. 'He's been gone fifteen minutes. This is ridiculous,' she snaps.

Joanna looks up and frowns. She joins Martha at the

window. 'Look at the clouds. Dappled grey and dirty white. God, we need the rain.'

'What do you think's happened to our artist?'

'His bag's still here,' Joanna says. 'You don't suppose he's had a heart attack?'

They run through the possibilities, canvassing the prospect of Roy slumped in the toilet after suffering a stroke or bent double behind the wheel of his car. They wait forty-five minutes before raising the alarm.

ROY IS FOUND that night, trudging along the road to the south coast, oblivious to the rain bucketing down. Canberra is desperate for a downpour, but not a single drop falls in the city's catchments.

The patrol officer who picked Roy up tells Beth that her husband was waterlogged but had his wits about him.

There is a brief item in the paper the next day, 'Artist Goes Walkabout'. Mora decides not to clip it. Her eyes alight on an adjacent report about a Japanese man who has become a father at the age of ninety-six. There is news, too, of another fissure in the Arctic shelf. She wipes a crumb from the corner of her mouth and decides to hide today's tidings from her houseguests.

BETH SITS AT Roy's bedside, cradling his hands. They're covered in sultana-sized sunspots and the skin puckers around his knuckles. Hands are like a birth certificate, she thinks, dating the vintage of people who cover their wrinkles in putty and plaster and a blush of fresh paint. Roy's hands have been roughened by his trade but they are beautiful to her, for the rough calluses and dirt-filled grooves.

The guest-room's clutter aggravates her sense of displacement. Old glass bottles blown by hand in blue and aqua and green gather dust on the mantelpiece. A painted china dalmatian sits on a royal blue cushion trimmed with gold tassels, its pointed snout dismissing a pair of black and white scotties on a gingham rug. Mora's daughter used to collect ornamental dogs; this was her room once.

Beth tries to gather her thoughts. She needs to retrieve their car from its parking spot outside the meteorological bureau. She needs to double-check the status of their private health insurance. She can only guess at the quality of their future.

She thinks of the physician and his wife who lay down on the floor of their apartment and administered a final exit. All their T's crossed: family and friends farewelled lavishly with French champagne and laughter; everything taken care of for the children; no one going through their underwear or letters and diaries; no arguments over possessions; no nursing home separation. She imagines Roy, incontinent and agitated, while she sits wheelchair bound, having finally surrendered Cuz. What other alternatives? Around-the-clock care at home, which they could never afford? A grafting operation to blend her sanity with his agility?

She will not ring the children. No need to frighten them. Anyway, there's nothing definite to tell. Roy will need to undergo tests and consultations. For weeks now she has buried her disquiet in the hope that his disorientation is a kink brought on by the strain of conception. The Canberra project is pressing in on him, she's told herself. It's been using up all the oxygen in his brain. Today she confronts the bleaker diagnosis. Dementia. Or a brain tumour. How will she manage the round of doctors' appointments? Their children work full-time and a diminishing circle of able-bodied friends have floated out on the tide of retirement to coastal towns, where the real estate is cheaper and life calmer.

The thoughts sluice through her head, raw and unprocessed. She has not given voice to any of them or sought Roy's counsel. Easier for now to deal with warmth and cold, hunger and thirst, which can be remedied easily. She barely slept last night. She wants Roy to take her in his arms, the way he used to when he would carry her to bed. She has come to rely on him: for shopping, transport, meals, hanging out the washing, cooking, endless chores. Boundless love.

Limbs and organs can be replaced. Knees, hips, hearts, lungs, kidneys, breasts: they've got a spare if you can bide the wait. But Roy, she fears, is losing bits of his being. Memory and presence of mind cannot be plucked from a dying man and rushed by ambulance to a gloved and gowned surgeon to be stitched inside another's skin. She could dress a wound or bandage a fracture, but how to live with a man who will become a stranger in his home and in her heart?

She takes a sip of cold tea and sees a single tear escape from the corner of Roy's eye, its salty path glistening. Using the sleeve of her cardigan, she dabs his face and he squeezes her hand.

'BRING ON A natural disaster,' says Harvey with relish, wheeling around from the bank of television monitors to kick off the morning conference. Janet, sitting with Jenny Monk at the far end of the table, hates the way he turns back the cuffs of his impeccably ironed shirt, the overripe smell of his aftershave.

'Doesn't have to be natural,' says Harvey's deputy. 'Any old disaster will do. A train crash. A little girl stuck down a hole. A race riot. A school shooting. A bridge collapse.'

'As long as your wife and kids aren't driving across at the time, right?' Jenny notes sharply.

'Come on, pay attention. This is not a hypothetical,' snarls Harvey.

Backs straighten and producers make algebraic entries in their notebooks.

'I could do a piece on renewed concerns over climate control. There are floods in northern Europe, and Melbourne had once-in-a-century rainfall last night,' offers Janet.

'Yeah,' Harvey says with a grin. 'We've got footage of cars floating around underground car parks. Looks like the crocodile tank at Sea World.'

'Great. And Phillip Bennett is ready to quit over government paralysis on warming,' she says.

'Who's Bennett?'

'Head of the meteorological bureau and chairman of the government's negotiating committee. But we've also got David Suzuki in town to promote his new —'

Harvey interrupts. 'Get Bennett. That could make news.'

Janet excuses herself, glad for an out. She heads downstairs for a coffee and falls into step with business reporter Linda Wallace.

'Notice anything?' Linda strikes a pose.

'You've lost weight,' says Janet diplomatically.

'Don't be ridiculous.'

'Um, new top?'

'Good God, girl, I thought you were a trained observer.' Linda points to her shoes. One is black suede with a gold buckle and the other is a red loafer. 'I was trying to decide which pair to wear when Matthew did a poo on the floor and I got distracted cleaning it up. I walk in here late and the security guys at reception are looking at my shoes and I'm thinking, Don't tell me I stepped in it.'

Janet laughs and they skip down the stairs, slipping into

easy conversation about the weekend, grateful for mutual support, for smalltalk about lunchboxes and toilet training amidst the subterfuge of office politics and current affairs.

'Roger worked all Saturday, then Sunday his office has a corporate team in the city triathlon,' Linda sighs. 'He gets home at seven thirty. I've fed the kids. We're halfway through baths, books and bed and he walks in, flicks on the tele and says, "What's for dinner?"'

'Nick's no better. He gave a presentation to a conference yesterday. He came home and slept most of the afternoon then gets up and says —'

'What's for dinner?'

'Worse than that,' says Janet. 'He comes into the kitchen, puts his arms around me and says, "How about it?"'

Back at her desk Janet calls up the wire service reports of the government's stand on climate control. The phone rings. Harry's in trouble: he punched James Amble in the face at recess. The third incident this term, Miss Dobbin reminds her, suggesting they meet later today. Janet rings Dale's office, for advice and solace, but she's busy with a patient. She looks out the window. The sky is heavy and darkening. Harry is sure to have noticed. His breath will quicken and become shallow as he imagines the rain pounding the windows until the glass breaks and the puddles broaden into rivers that will burst through levees and lap at the front door.

She drinks her coffee, which is cold. She thinks about medication and therapy, sees her son as a teenager, brooding and volatile. She imagines him slipping out of her care and drifting with a bad crowd, stealing cars, flirting with risk, surfing suburban trains, taking drugs, dropping out of school. Her chest tightens and she pictures him in an alley slumped against an overflowing garbage bin.

Appalled by the turn of her thoughts, she stops herself rafting the rapids of worst case scenarios. Harry's a happy, healthy lad. He just punched a kid. If peace prevailed in the playground, children would never grasp the art of conflict resolution and Miss Dobbin would be bored stiff. She rings Nick, but he can't rearrange his diary to meet her at the school.

'I meant to tell you,' he says, 'I had a chat to Simon Calvert. He was giving a paper yesterday so I introduced myself. He remembers Harry, at least he said he did. I think we need to go back to him. He's sold on the benefits of medication, says seventy per cent of children do better at school on stimulants.'

Up against hard statistics, her fears sound flimsy, so she says nothing. Only last week one of the specialist teachers stopped her in the street after drop-off to recommend that she talk with other parents in the same boat. Janet could picture this boat, one of those ferries that are always sinking. The teacher told her that twenty of the school's two hundred students had been diagnosed with Attention Deficit Hyperactivity Disorder.

Dale said these figures weren't so surprising, not in an affluent suburb where teachers are rewarded for prompt diagnosis of less than perfect development and parents can afford to pay for enhancement.

Early intervention cuts against Janet's belief in letting be. How can they standardise concentration and energy? Harry's just a boy. Vigorous, exuberant, active. What's wrong with the teachers that they can't manage her son?

She points the bone her way. What's wrong with you? Why didn't you see fit to stay home with him from the beginning? Get up now. Go on – walk out of here and be there for him.

A message flashes on her screen from Harvey. 'Any luck with Bennett?'

She is angry at Harvey, at Harry, at herself. She thinks of Linda cleaning up poo and how easy mothering would be if the problems could be wiped away with disinfectant. There is no point in appealing to Harvey – he's on to his third family. Children are dispensable. His loyalties lie with the company, the third wife, the career.

She feels her own loyalty slipping away as she emails him a small lie. 'Bennett's tied up all day. I'm trying for tomorrow.'

Across the newsroom, pictures of floods in northern Italy flash across the bank of screens. Several of her colleagues stop and watch footage of a young boy being swept along in torrential brown water. Miraculously, his jacket snags on a telegraph pole and he grabs it with both arms as the reporters cheer and whoop.

Janet gets up from her chair to take in the drama. Why hasn't the cameraman stepped in to rescue the boy, who is now shimmying slowly up the pole? He has a gash in his right leg. Below in the swirling water a shopping trolley bobs. The console switches feeds and her phone rings.

It's Phillip Bennett. 'I'm free at two thirty. Where do you want to meet?'

'Tomorrow would suit me a whole lot better,' she begs.

'I might not be in the job tomorrow,' he whispers, casting his line.

This better be good, Janet thinks, picking up the phone to reschedule the conference with Miss Dobbin.

That night her story on Bennett's resignation leads the news bulletin. He said he could no longer serve a government happy to denigrate science for political ends, a government that thinks the warming is a conspiracy fuelled by environmentalists, a government obsessed with cultural wars. Look at the evidence, he had told the prime minister. Listen to the scientists. But when he sought support for climate modelling and monitoring, there was no money in the budget. No leadership in international forums. No spine.

But what will stay with viewers is the face of the eight-year-old boy from Siena. In his excitement at the arrival of a rescue helicopter, he lets go of the pole he has been hugging and tumbles and falls headfirst into the muddy water coursing beneath him.

Janet cruises home on a rush of adrenaline but as she takes the front steps two at a time she hears Mel's tearful screams, punishment for her lateness.

'I hate you, Harry,' Mel sobs, disappearing into her room as Janet enters to see Harry flying in the direction of his, banging his door so furiously that a spray of plaster dusts the floor.

She goes to Mel first, to learn that Harry has given his sister's favourite doll a crewcut with nail scissors.

Jasmin is in the kitchen, washing dishes to make a quick getaway. 'They've been pretty good until now.' She shrugs, wiping her hands on the tea towel before grabbing her gear. She's done her bit: homework completed, children fed and bathed. Jasmin is like the cleaner who used to line up Janet's shoes in perfectly straight rows but never scrubbed the grime between the bathroom tiles. The cat's insistent meow from the back door confirms other chores and needs unmet.

Janet tries to enter Harry's room.

'Go away,' he shouts, holding the door shut.

'Open up.' Janet pushes until she wins the struggle. Harry flings himself face down on his bed.

'Don't you want any friends? Don't you want anyone to play with you? Why do you think no one ever asks you over?'

she shouts, wishing immediately that she could retract her words.

'Leave me alone!' he screams.

She sits next to him, attempting peace with a tousle of his curls, but he buries his face into the pillow. The dreamcatcher he made from recycled ribbons and blackbird feathers floats on a breeze sneaking in through the open window.

'I wish I could promise that her hair will grow back,' Janet says, when she looks in on her daughter. Only last week Mel had boxed up her dolls to make room for the trinkets of a girl approaching her teens; the one with long hair had been the sole survivor of this cleansing.

'I wish I didn't have Harry for a brother.'

'Cassie did something like this to me once.'

Mel perks up, interested. 'What?'

'She cut my donkey bear up. She said she was giving it a heart transplant, saving its life. I'd slept with Donkey every night since I could remember, and I wanted to chop Cassie into bits. Mum took Donkey to be mended but they put too much stuffing back inside him and he was never quite the same.'

'What did Grandma do to Cassie?'

'She tried to take Cassie's teddy away as punishment but Cassie screamed until she turned blue. She talked to me about how life was harder for my sister because . . .'

She trails off, trying to remember how her mother had

explained Cassie's rages. But in the end no one could explain them, let alone Cassie herself, and no doctor, teacher or other guardian ever thought to forward the prognosis of a syndrome or disorder to make sense of her behaviour, her character, her moods.

When Cassie finally flung off the restraints of school and home, their parents worried every time the phone rang – had the worst finally happened? Was she in the clink, ten feet under, in intensive care, or simply short of a quid? Gradually they adjusted to the novel idea that however perilous her state of independence, however unconventional and crackpot her life, she managed to survive on her own, never happier than when snubbing their timidity. Janet is conscious of her pale experiences beside Cassie's vagabond existence. Her sister sleeps under the occasional bridge, cadges food from supermarket bins, travels unencumbered, leaping from stone to stone across the rapid flowing river of her life.

Mel gives voice to Janet's next thought. 'Is Harry like Cassie?'

Janet bats back the answer, doesn't miss a beat. 'No. Not at all.' She picks up Mel's doll and considers her plight. 'We could crop the lot, streak it and get her a nose pin. A punk? She'd be the only one of her kind.'

Mel shakes her head. Difference does not become a conformist.

'We'll see about getting a new one,' Janet promises.

She runs upstairs to change her clothes before returning to the mad barber. His room is empty and the window open. The last time Harry fled, he went no further than the jacaranda tree out the back, fettered by his fears.

'HOW IS HE?' Mora asks, as Beth's slurred footsteps announce her approach.

'He hasn't spoken a single word,' Beth says quietly, taxying Cuz around the kitchen table, which is cluttered with newspapers and pens and spectacles cases. She lowers herself on to an old church pew, looking first for a cushion to soften the seat. Her hips throb with pain.

'Let him rest,' says Mora. 'He must have walked for hours last night.' Her eyes drop compulsively to the cryptic crossword on her lap.

The suggestion that Roy needs nothing more than a lie-down is a duplicitous convenience Beth conspires with for the momentary peace it brings.

'Besides,' confides Mora, 'I can't even have a bowel movement until I've got at least two clues out.'

Beth manages a smile at this. 'I've always meant to take up cryptics,' she says, envious of Mora's busy silence, her hand scribbling as she unscrambles an anagram.

'I just don't know what to do,' she whispers, flummoxed by the disarray of her existence.

'It's easy once you get a handle on the clues.' Mora's eyes are glued to seven down.

'No. About Roy.'

'Of course,' says Mora guiltily, putting her pen down.

Last night she'd dreamed of holding an exhibition in the great hall of Parliament House. Minutes before the opening, she discovered that the title cards were blank and when she tried to write them by hand, she couldn't remember how to spell. There but for the grace of God go I, she thought on opening her eyes. She wishes that she could dig up a plan to set Roy right, but the little she knows of his recent undoing discourages her.

She reaches across the table to clasp Beth's hand. 'How about I make us a pot of coffee? We need something stronger than Earl Grey.'

'I could do with a brandy.'

'What do you think is going on with him?' Mora asks as she fills the blackened kettle at the sink.

Beth sits silently, unwilling to speak the name of the bogey stalking Roy. She pulls a mohair rug over her knees. She is cold to the bones, even though the sun is up and drying puddles of rain.

Finally she speaks. 'This is a big commission for him, his last major public work. It's hard for me to comprehend the magnitude of that. Of course he's overwrought, but this isn't the first time he's been swamped. I think I've been in denial. We both have, hoping like hell it will pass.'

'And it might,' says Mora. She takes two blue mugs from her cupboard and a jug for milk.

'It might,' echoes Beth. 'But I'm not so sure after last night's turn.'

Mora grinds the beans by hand and stands at the kitchen window, waiting for the kettle's whistle. The lavender needs a trim, she thinks.

Beth makes her own inventory of jobs. 'We should see a specialist when we get back to Sydney,' she says, mind skipping back and forth from minor inconveniences to catastrophic obstacles. How will they drive back to Sydney? Can Roy finish his sculpture? 'What about you? Have you noticed anything strange about Roy?'

Mora dithers. No, yes, no, yes. Like stepping from sunlight into the cool of a curtained room, she needs time to get her bearings. 'As I've said before, we all get white-outs. Little things that might mean nothing.'

'What kind of things?'

'The other night he seemed confused when we were talking about the past. And recently when we've spoken, it's like he's slipping in and out of the conversation. Once he even left me hanging on the phone.'

Beth cannot betray Roy by confirming these lapses with other examples. They fall into silence as Mora spreads ricotta thickly on toast and sprinkles the slices with cinnamon. Beth is ravenous. She chews hungrily and her tongue loosens. 'Isn't dementia supposed to affect your short-term memory?'

'Yes,' says Mora. 'I think that's right. But a woman from my bridge club, her husband went through this and . . .' She hesitates, unwilling to recount that towards the end, when the man was in a dementia unit, he remembered their old dog but not the wife at the other end of the leash.

'Go on,' prods Beth, helping herself to a second slice.

'I was just going to say that nothing happens overnight. If you detect dementia early enough, you can stabilise it with medication.'

'But he's always been so fit. I've had ailments for both of us. And now the terrible thing is . . .' It's Beth's turn to pause, but she forces herself forward. 'Sometimes I think I would rather Roy die than watch him being buried alive.'

Mora's shock is evident in the fix of her gaze. 'You're jumping ahead of yourself. He's had a few memory lapses and a very long walk, but he's conscious of everything around him. Surely that's a good sign?'

'Has he said anything to you, Mora?'

'Not a whisper.' Which is near enough to what passed between them the other night. Mora isn't prepared to let on to the extent of her own fears for Roy.

Beth suppresses the thoughts that dart through her depths, feeding on flakes of despair. Mora studies a crossword clue and toys with a solution.

Beth speaks eventually. 'Remember when your father had a stroke and we were sitting here at this table? You were roasting peppers. I was peeling the skin off and you told me to leave some of it on, for the texture, and I snapped at you. "How can you worry about what the peppers look like when your father's dying?" And Roy said that he wouldn't want to survive a stroke if it left him impaired. Do you remember?'

Beth has tears running down her face. 'You can manage the disintegration of the body – I wouldn't recommend it, but you can get by. You can go on. But this is worse. It's not a white-out, Mora, this is blackness.'

Mora reaches out to her friend. 'I don't know anyone our age who isn't worried about losing their grip. You say now that you wouldn't want to live, and you mean it, but how do you know what you can bear? Look at John Bayley saying that Iris Murdoch was happy watching *Teletubbies*. How do we know she wasn't content with her lot?' Mora knows she's babbling. 'What about my friend, the pharmacist? The one who swore she wouldn't go through radiation or chemotherapy? When she was diagnosed with lymphoma, she tried every medical missile she could lay her hands on.'

'You've told me that story, and I know why you're telling it to me again.'

Mora is quietly relieved at Beth's verbal cuff.

'Help me see the bright side here,' Beth pleads, her old self struggling to the surface.

'Okay.' Mora perks up at the prospect of a game. 'If it's what you think it is, at least you'll qualify for a disabled parking sticker.' They both giggle.

'We already have one,' snorts Beth.

'Well, you won't have to worry about repeating yourself.' And Roy will forget about your affair with —'

'Mora!' Beth's spine stiffens with indignation.

A door opening in the hall diverts their attention. They listen to the shuffle of feet and then the sound of Roy's piss hitting the porcelain, alert for any misstep in this perfunctory deed. The toilet flushes and their eyes catch each other's embarrassment and relief. They hear the scrape of the cantankerous hot water tap, then the clank of metal on the tiled floor.

'Bugger,' Roy curses.

Mora knocks into Cuz as she lurches forth to help Roy, who is on his knees scrabbling after the tap handle, his withered scrotum swinging between his legs. He uses the bath edge to lever himself upright and leans towards her with a forwardness that surprises her. But still she is not ready for the hand that snakes up and tweaks her breast.

DRAWN BY THE ocean's promise, Roy loves the descent from Canberra to the south coast. The prospect of visiting Billy, who's going to snatch an hour off work to spend with them, is a bonus that makes the trip close to perfect.

Roy has found his way back into the world without further mishap, except that he seems somehow more vivid to Beth, as if he is daring her to doubt his homecoming.

On Saturday they went to the market and bought aubergines with deep purple skins that shone like polished boots in a military parade. Roy cooked ratatouille. No one mentioned Friday night. Not once. Not even Phillip Bennett, who Roy insisted on inviting around to dinner that night, along with a National Gallery curator who is convening an exhibition of early Australian sculpture. 'Here's to a sustainable future,' Roy said, by way of grace, adding, 'for all of us,' in quiet amen.

At first Mora and Beth were so stunned by his embrace of the morning, they turned their backs on pointless rounds of second guessing. Mora boxed up the memory of her encounter with Roy in the bathroom, but she kept wanting to adjust his volume, turn him down.

This morning he collected the car, crabby at the women asking if he was okay to drive. Mora waves them off by throwing an old shoe after the car, for good luck, in keeping with an odd family custom.

Beth plans to broach Friday night with Roy before they reach Braidwood and begin the dangerous zig-zag descent of Clyde Mountain. But the longer she lets it lie, the more uncertain she becomes. If he is suffering insecurity, then he needs her unconditional support.

The road's steep decline requires concentration. As they approach Government Bend, Roy applauds the wit of whoever was responsible for signposting this impossible curve that slows traffic to a crawl. 'A bureaucrat? Or one of the labourers. What do you think?'

She laughs, telling herself to relax and enjoy him; stop doubting his cheerfulness. Wait for him to speak first.

A pelican guards the jetty at sleepy Nelligen, where they cross the bridge over the Clyde River. The postcard prettiness of weatherboard cottages standing beside calm water soothes Beth's disquiet. The car climbs briefly and through the tall gums beside the road she tracks the river as it widens to meet the sea at Batemans Bay.

Seagulls flock around the fish and chip shop, bickering over a greasy white paper cocoon that one has pulled from the rubbish bin and ripped open. The strip of shops in the main street, selling surf gear and tourist gifts, looks just as hungry for crumbs of retail trade.

Lillipilli Aged Care Lodge is set in bush a short distance off the highway. Roy asks whether he's taken the right turn, which he has, and just past a sign pointing the way to a crematorium is a circular driveway that sweeps in front of the lodge. They ring the buzzer at the entrance; a sudden whip of birdsong lingers gloriously. Billy appears, punching the keypad to open his fortress, making a noisy fuss of them both. He hugs Roy and gives Beth a kiss on each cheek. 'Come and meet my deputy, Anton.'

Billy has told Beth about Anton, a surfer who rides the ward like a shore break, taking whatever is served up. She half expects to see boardshorts and sandals under the young man's pale green cotton smock. Male nurses are not so common but one of the sassier patients in Billy's care tells whoever will listen that Florence Nightingale was not a patch on these blokes. Beth knows her son shows more kindness than relatives can sustain towards fathers, aunts, sisters or a circle of in-laws who have grown misshapen and agitated, unable to remember visitors.

Beth and Roy are introduced to Nance, a wanderer clad in

thick black woollen socks, who has the habit of clambering in and out of other people's beds at night. This adventuring has resulted in several fractures, when her hosts rolled over to make room for the intruder and fell on to the floor. She registers Roy and Beth as nothing more than a roadblock in her circular lap of the corridors.

Billy stops to get his jacket from the office and Beth notices on his desk the perfectly round thunder rock that Roy brought home from an outback trip. The rock was cored like an apple to hold the red and blue feather of a rosella. Roy had tied a blindfold over Billy's eyes so that he could feel each object and guess at its secrets.

Roy, too, has spotted the rock and cups it in his hands. 'I remember finding this,' he says.

Nance follows them out to the security door that marks the exit. A group of patients stand silently there, like dairy cows waiting outside a milking shed. Billy shepherds aside a stooped man who rests his weight on one leg as he rubs the threads of his shrunken jumper between thumb and forefinger.

'C'mon, Rupe,' Billy coos into the man's purple-veined ear.

Rupert used to be a teacher, he tells them as they drive into town for lunch beside the river. 'He gets into trouble with the other residents because he's always shuffling their chairs around in front of the tele.'

'Probably blocking their view,' Beth says.

'No, they get cranky because they like occupying the same chair in the same place day in, day out and Rupert disturbs the order.'

'Does he have family?' she asks, curious at Rupert's flicker of rebellion.

'He's got a nephew, I know that much. The nephew's got a red dot on Rupert's most valuable possession, a program from the Beatles' Australian tour autographed by John Lennon. He'll be waiting years to collect. Rupert's as strong as an ox.'

'How does he fill his days?' Beth asks, but she can already make a good enough guess.

'He gets dressed. He eats in the dining room. He sits. He spends hours by the door. Watches tele.'

'And how long do you think he can live like this?'

'It all depends. A simple hip fracture often triggers complications. Pneumonia. Dementia'll kill him eventually.'

They order grilled fillets of rockling and salad and find a table beside a window overlooking the mouth of the bay and the parade of fishing boats and gulls. Beth is surprised by news of Billy's lovelife, which Roy extracts inadvertently with a question about his guitar.

'I have been playing a bit, yeah. Matter of fact, I've written two new songs. I've met a girl with a beautiful voice, the daughter of the guy who runs the funeral parlour. She works there.' He shifts a curtain of dark brown curls with fingers that are long like Roy's. Fine boned, with his father's olive skin, he is a handsome man, Beth thinks. He has a mole on his left cheek and two on his neck, which she checks habitually for changes in size and texture, all part of the maternal once-over. And though he has been clean for nine years, she makes herself look for trackmarks on the inside of his arms. At thirty-eight he has a knack for disastrous relationships, but she keeps hoping love will visit him.

'She's a Buddhist,' he volunteers. 'And she's got two grown-up children.'

Roy catches a sigh in Beth's acknowledgement, and distracts her by pointing to a bulldozer clearing land across the river.

'Retirement units,' Billy tells them. 'I've put a down payment on one for the two of you.'

Roy chuckles appropriately.

They drop Billy back at the lodge, and Beth notes that Rupert hasn't shifted from his spot by the door. She imagines his days as the seasons pass and years go by, waiting for the nephew to drop by or to send a card every once in a while. They pass through a bus stop of a coastal town, and as Roy slows down to observe the speed limit she makes a promise. She will spare her man this.

ROY ROUNDS THE corner into the back lane, surprised by new signs of fortification in a neighbourhood where his right of way was once rarely questioned. Now, solid brick fences are built for privacy and garages are remote controlled. Everything buttoned down tight. No loose pickets or flapping gates. No rusty corrugated roofs. He peers over a shoulder-high rendered wall, into a paved courtyard with raked white stones. A bush has been clipped fastidiously into the letter A. Ashley? Armageddon? Arsehole? Rogue vulgarities are leaking into his language and he likes their shock value. He told Beth his gonads were playing up last night, and she flinched.

The panic and fear that used to flood through him after every stumble has begun to ebb as he grows accustomed to sliding back and forth between two states of mind. On a clear day he worries whether he can execute the masterpiece he thinks is taking shape. He has been scavenging materials, visiting demolition sites, the tip, raking nature strips on the eve of household waste collections and casing the streets at dusk, propelled by a restlessness he can't fathom.

The ramshackle piles of refuse collected behind his studio speak of water. There is the clawed foot from an old bath, coated in layers of white paint. A shower rose big enough to soak three people at once. A hot-water bottle still tucked inside its hand-knitted woollen coat. A hospital bedpan. He found a discarded life jacket on a ferry pier and wore it home. The straw hat he souvenired that same day now hangs above his chair. Outside the council crêche he nabbed a discarded fishtank with a tiny china pagoda.

Beth had alerted him to the brass taps, two marked 'hot' and one 'cold', left lying out the front of the old boarding house that she passed every week on her way to meet Dale. The building was bulldozed between Fridays. One week she waved to the two old men sunning on the verandah and seven days later the site had been razed and the rubble combed into furrows. The men used to sit on plastic milk crates nicked from the mixed goods shop across the road. The Asian man behind the counter kept a cheerful eye on these toothless natives, slinging them daily handouts of stale muffins and blackened bananas. Beth sometimes saw the men scurrying across the road, in various states of undress, loot tucked under their arms. Age lent a dignity to circumstances that would demean younger drifters. 'Hello darlin',' they'd chorus when she ambled by. She'd even got to know one of them a little. He looked at least a hundred but was five years her junior.

She'd hoped Roy might find out what had happened to the men, but all he brought back were the taps and a length of copper piping twisted and bent from being ripped off a wall. Their vanishing disturbed her. Beth asked the shopkeeper if he knew where the men now lived but he shook his head.

On the site, new townhouses are being built, for young professionals who will not be idling out front to watch the sun travel across the sky.

Roy finds another fence to peep over, bewitched by the absence of clutter. No sign of a shed. He spots a cast-iron birdbath, like the one his grandmother had under the crab apple tree in her back yard. Rusted brown, the dish is round and shallow with a weathervane for the birds to perch on. He tries the gate but there is no handle. He looks along the lane for a couple of loose bricks or a bin to help him up and over, and does not notice the police patrol car watching from the road. He commandeers a green wheelie bin from one end of the lane and clambers on top. As he leans over the wall a blue light under the eaves of the house begins to flash and a siren shrieks. He tries to scramble down but slips and is caught by the two policewomen who finished their takeaway coffees in the car while waiting for him to strike.

The older of the two women sees the fright in Roy's eyes

and senses that a computer check will reveal nothing more sinister on his record than parking fines.

He trembles, confused by the wailing alarm and the closeness of the women who lead him towards the car. He wants the birdbath. He shakes free but can't rid himself of the hands and fingers that crawl over him, pulling at his jumper to get their suckers into his flesh. The effort of beating them off makes him hot and breathless and he curses as the women intensify their attack. Throwing his head back, he feels spits of water on his face. The sensation calms him.

'Come on,' says the older officer, urging Roy into the back of the car, 'before it pours.'

The younger cop recognises his disorientation. He reminds her of the stranger she calls Mum. Before her mother required full-time care, she took to roaming the streets, pulled this way and that by restlessness. What is it about sundown, the policewoman wonders, and the body clocks of people who are unwinding?

DALE LADDERS HER tights on a tendril of climbing rose that has come loose from the trellis arching over the path to Janet's front door. Sydney is succulent after the wettest winter month on record. A football lies discarded on the ground like rotten fruit, its bladder torn. She picks up the bike helmet that has been dropped two strides away on the soggy ground, unsurprised by the name scrawled in red paint on the crown. At the end of a muddy skid, a battered two-wheeler has been left where it fell, handlebars twisted. It's all too chaotic for her taste. A professional who encourages people to expose themselves, she keeps her own seams tightly stitched.

Dinner was Janet's idea. Grateful for Dale's help with Harry, she and Nick have decided to return the favour by introducing her to a hand-picked, eligible man.

Arranged dinner dates invariably disappoint. After her most recent attempt, with a life coach who'd confessed after two glasses of wine to being bisexual, Dale told herself 'never again' and withdrew her carefully crafted profile from an online site where the unattached look for love. She warned Janet, who persuaded her that making up a foursome with the American researcher visiting Nick's clinic was a civic duty consistent with Dale's support for the US alliance.

Even though she suspected a dud, Dale deliberated over her wardrobe, wearing lingerie and make-up, which she applied with care for the first time in her life. They'd agreed to meet at Janet's place and then walk around the corner to the local pub's spiffy brasserie.

A gentle knock on the door brings no one so she gives a harder rap, which summons running feet and Janet's welcome as she wipes floury hands on a butcher's apron. They kiss and Dale does her best to avoid a set of white fingerprints on her black dress. 'I thought we were eating out?' she says, looking at her host's kitchen wear.

'We are. I'm just making the kids pizzas. Harry's helping me.'

Harry stands on an upside down saucepan, decorating his oval of dough with salami, cheese and tomato.

'Yum,' Dale says encouragingly, from a safe distance.

'Where's the pineapple?' he demands.

Janet fetches a can from the pantry.

'Let me open it,' he insists. 'On my own,' he adds, as Janet puts out a hand to steady the can, which tips, spilling a sticky yellow mush on the tiled floor.

'I wanted pineapple rings,' he quarrels, ignoring the mess.

'This is pineapple, but it's been chopped up,' Janet explains firmly, as Nick arrives, scrubbed clean. He escorts Dale into the living room, an oasis of neatness either rarely used or spruced especially for guests. Framed photographs of the children as babies and on their first day at school are perched on the white mantelpiece. Nick closes the door, muffling the kitchen concerto. He opens a bottle of white wine, chatting easily. Filling their glasses, he toasts health and happiness and puts on a CD that Dale has been meaning to buy. Neither of them hear the low growl of thunder rolling in over eastern Sydney.

Harry abandons his pizza-making efforts, to Janet's relief. She slides the pizzas into the oven, washes her hands and goes to check on the children. Mel is in her room, reading the eleventh book in a fantasy sequel, and Harry is watching the weather channel. Here's his big chance to watch an MA rated movie and instead he is engrossed by nature. She pauses in front of the screen for a report on flash flooding in Indonesia and the northern Philippines, pictures of children clambering on rooftop pontoons to escape rising tides.

Taking the remote from his lap, Janet switches over to cartoons. Aware of a strengthening wind outside, she closes the window.

'I like the window open,' Harry says, flicking back to the weather channel.

In the living room she finds Dale and Nick inspecting the CD collection and orders a tank-sized goblet of wine.

'Who's babysitting?' Dale asks.

'The neighbours have a lovely Year Twelve girl who Mel adores, one of those all-rounders who excel at everything. Come to think of it, she's a clone of you twenty years ago.'

Dale smiles. 'Bet she's not half as ravishing.'

'She's gorgeous, but you might pip her in the personality stakes. The funny thing is, all she wants to do is get married. Her mother is plotting to kill the boyfriend.'

'This is sounding very familiar,' Dale says. 'That's what Mum threatened when I told her I wanted to defer my uni course and follow Emil Bonner to London.'

'He had such a crush on you. What's he doing now?'

'He's a lawyer, I think. Someone told me he's married with four children, almost all grown.'

'Four children?' Janet groans, as if Dale had said forty.

'Yes, and I'll be lucky to have one.'

Nick notices the clench of her fingers around the stem of the glass.

'Who knows, maybe you'll get together with a guy who brings his own kids. A BYO,' Janet laughs. She takes another slug of wine, then frowns and jumps to her feet. 'The pizzas!'

Nick follows her into the kitchen. 'You are so insensitive,' he whispers.

She stares at him blankly. 'What have I done now?'

'Dale wants a child of her own, and all you've got to say to her is that maybe she'll get lucky with someone else's kids?'

Janet turns her back on him. 'You don't know the first thing about how Dale and I talk to each other.' She takes the pizzas – slightly burnt – from the oven. 'Anyway, where's Warren got to? Don't tell me he's going to stand Dale up.'

As she speaks the phone rings and Janet picks up the receiver before Nick can get to it. It's Harvey's voice at the other end of the line. 'Drop whatever you're doing. We need you on deck.'

His urgency rivets her. 'What's the problem?'

'This storm's smashed half of Sydney to smithereens. Hasn't it hit you yet?'

'No.' Janet peers out the window. 'But the wind's lifting.'

'Tell your hubby to lock down tight at home and get yourself to work pronto.'

'I can't, I've got guests.'

Harvey doesn't hear her. 'Jesus, you should see the damage. Hailstones the size of cricket balls, I'm not kidding. Cars have been pummelled flat. All our skylights have been smashed. It's a freaking war zone out here.'

Janet can hear the faint call of emergency sirens in the distance. 'Harvey, I'm sorry.'

'Sorry isn't an option —'

His phone is cut dead. Janet tries ringing him back but the call is diverted just as Harry cannons into her, pyjama top pulled over his head like a chador. 'It's storming on the television, Mum.' His voice is high, quavery. He can hardly breathe.

Janet lifts him up and holds him tight. She looks at Nick. 'They want me at work. I have to go.'

Nick stares at her if she's just said that she wants both legs amputated.

'Don't go. Don't leave me,' Harry keens. 'There's going to be a flood. Are we all going to drown?'

Janet strokes his face, tender. 'You know Dad and I will never let anything bad happen to you or to Mel.' She passes Harry into Nick's arms. 'I'll be as quick as I can.'

'Sure you will,' Nick says tersely, then turns and carries Harry to his bedroom.

Dale finds them there, after helping Janet locate her keys and soothing her guilt at leaving her son and guest. The boy stares out the window, wide eyes taking in trees bent by the wind, his weathervanes. He imagines water swallowing solid ground, flushing climbers out of canyons like daddy-long-legs shot down the bath's plughole. He chews a threadbare piece of pale-blue cotton blanket, his breathing shallow.

Dale puts a quiet hand on Nick's shoulders. 'Your friend Warren called. He's staying home to mop up storm damage.'

A thin smile from Nick. 'And so ends another blissful night at six Wattletree Avenue.'

He goes downstairs to fix them some kind of dinner, and Dale sits on Harry's bed. 'How about you come and curl up here and I'll tell you a story?'

Harry shakes his head. He winds the strand of blanket closer around his wrist and rubs a pinch of it between his fingers. Dale can see that this is an elaborate ritual, getting this worried bit of cloth just right.

She joins him at the window but when she goes to pull the curtains shut, he hisses at her.

'Don't. They have to stay open. I have to check on the sky.'

'Why is that?'

'Because it's going wrong.' He takes a ragged breath, and does his best to explain. 'We have to wear hats in the playground because there's a hole in the sky. The hole's making the sea get bigger and there's all these gases in the air making the world hotter. The weather's off its rocker.'

Dale had been spooked herself that morning by reports of Venetian gondoliers who can't fit their boats under the city's bridges, because of higher tides. 'Do you know anyone who has drowned in a flood?' she asks Harry.

He thinks for a moment. 'No.'

'Do you know anyone who has been hit by lightning?'

His brow crinkles. 'No.'

'I don't either.' She smiles, reassuring.

'But what about the pictures on television? They don't lie. What about the tsunami?'

'Things like that don't happen here. Your mum and dad will always look after you.'

He throws her a disbelieving look. 'They can't stop the bad things happening.'

'Maybe not always. But has anything bad ever happened to them?'

Harry ponders on this, then shakes his head. 'No.'

'Then why do you think scary things are ever going to happen to you?'

He stares at her, bemused, the storm outside the window temporarily forgotten. She takes his hand and leads him to his bed, and this time he doesn't pull back. She folds down his rainbow-patterned doona and he slides in.

'Do you have any kids?'

'No.' Her answer's hopelessly incomplete.

'Why not?'

Even though he's told her of his monsters, she can't open up to him. 'I just got busy doing other things. But maybe one day I will.'

Harry snuggles down and she listens to the quietening rhythm of his breath. If her nerve holds, and her aging ovaries perform on cue, there is still a chance, a flimsy prospect, a kite-tail of hope to carry her forward.

Harry has gone to sleep, his fingers relaxing their grip on the blanket. She rises gently from the bed. The floorboards creak but his jaw slackens as she sidles out the door.

Nick is in the living room, nursing a full glass of wine as he watches Janet on the plasma screen. She's cloaked in an electric-blue jacket, anchoring live crosses from Paddington to Bundeena. Residents are sloshing through living rooms, shocked by the weather's vengeance. 'We thought we were being invaded,' a middle-aged man says, standing outside the ruin of his house. 'It sounded like low-flying aircraft at first, then these ice balls dropped out of the sky like bombs.'

Dale sits next to Nick on the couch and they watch Janet together without a word, until her mobile bleats at her. It's a friend calling to report that she's lost half her roof. When Dale hangs up, the phone signals that she has voicemail.

'Darling, it's your crippled old mother. I hope you're not out in a boat. Could you ring me when you get home?'

Beth's voice is calm, but even so Dale detects consternation. She calls her parents but there's no reply.

Nick hugs her at the front door. 'Ring when you get home, okay? Let me know you're safe.'

WEAVING IN AND out of back streets in the darkness, Dale is stunned at how the storm has struck at random, clobbering the harbour's northern rim. Her windscreen wipers are pathetic in the pelting rain. She swerves to avoid a candy-striped umbrella cartwheeling on to the road, lashed by the wind. She calls home, but again the number rings out. Around the corner from the cafe where she and Beth rendezvous for coffee, a Moreton bay fig has fallen on power lines. An emergency worker in an orange vest waves her back and she slips down a narrow laneway, desperate now to reach her parents. At the top of their street she sees a hooded figure hoisting a wooden oar over one shoulder. It's Roy.

Dale pulls up alongside him and slides down the passenger window, shouting to get his attention. But he stares at her distrustfully, as if she's a stranger.

'Dad? Dad, are you okay?'

Switching the oar to his other shoulder, he marches away

without a word towards home, rain whipping at his back.

By the time she pulls up outside, he's disappeared into the studio. Head down, she dashes through the rain and knocks on the front door, but there's no reply. She finds the spare key and lets herself in, stepping over a pile of rolled-up newspapers, still wrapped in plastic, lying on the hallway floor. She gropes for the light switch but the power is out.

'Mum?' She feels her way forward, distinguishing familiar landmarks from slovenly additions that are strange and unwelcome. Unwashed jars and takeaway containers line the floor around the rubbish bin. The sink is stacked full of dirty plates and cups. In the lounge room underpants, stockings and socks are spread out to dry along the top of the sofa. It's only two weeks since Dale last visited but the house is squalid. It smells in here. She trips over a green garbage bag as she heads out the back door, calling out to her mother. She can hear the scrape of Beth's walking frame over by Roy's studio.

She rushes out to shepherd Beth back indoors, throwing her arms around shoulders that sag. 'Are you all right?'

Beth just nods, too worn to yell. Her thick white hair is sopping, the clothes peg pinned to the hem of her grubby floral nightie as out of place as the oar on Roy's shoulder. Beth has shed weight and she seems frail as Dale steers her towards the house.

She should've known better than to track her parents' wellbeing with phone calls. When they were kids, Beth would disguise any domestic ugliness with a honeyed greeting to whoever might call. Now Dale, too, has been hoodwinked by her mother's conviviality. 'Are you okay, Mum?' she asks, as she settles Beth into an armchair.

'I'm fine,' Beth whispers.

Not since the night of Billy's overdose has Dale seen such brokenness at home.

Roy went crazy then, smashing his son's shell collection, the one cherishable Billy had not been able to pawn for dope. Beth had retrieved the shards and later Roy laid them into a clenched fist he modelled from clay. That's how Roy spoke to them, through the magpie thieving of bits and pieces – bark, pods, glass, and now an oar.

Dale finds candles and dry clothes and tucks her mother up in a satin quilt. The power surges back on and she glances out the back door to Roy's studio, comforted to see golden light pouring out of the windows. The studio has always been off-limits to visitors. When he is happy with a work in progress, he invites Beth to view it in his absence, at an appointed time. They'd agreed to this procedure after a terrible row early in their marriage, when he accused Beth of sabotaging him with a glib response to his art. Since that day, she sets out her comments on paper and delivers them to the studio steps, weighted down by a rock or a pine cone.

'I spoke to Dad in the street before, but he wouldn't answer me. What was he doing out in the storm?' Dale sets to making an omelette as she speaks.

'He's always roamed at night, you know that.' Beth's voice is small. 'Even the night you were born, he went on one of his treks. There was a full moon and he collected feathers. He walked all the way from Coogee to Bondi and around Centennial Park. He was creating his sculpture for the children's hospital, his first commission.'

Dale knows that the piece they nicknamed 'The Nest' is the one Beth loves most. Roy constructed it out of copper ribbons which he wove into a giant mesh bowl. Names of children sewn back together, as well as the names of those who were not, are engraved into the copper. Tiny models of toys and trees, birds and fantasy creatures are threaded through the ribbons like charms on a bracelet. Parents who have lost children come to visit on anniversaries, to leave behind letters or flowers. Sometimes they tie bows to the sculpture, cut from clothing, in remembrance. Stuffed toys are left at its base.

A thud carries from the studio. Beth and Dale freeze, heads cocked, eyes narrowed, interpreting what they can hear above the rain.

'I'm thinking I might stay for a few days, just to give you and Dad a hand around the place. What do you think?' Dale asks.

Beth shrugs, still listening for sounds of Roy. 'I was so worried about him tonight that I looked inside the studio.' Her face crumples and she covers it with the tea towel she has been folding and refolding into tiny squares.

Dale takes her hand. 'Hey, Mum, don't cry.'

It takes Beth a minute or two to compose herself. She exhales slowly. 'I've been watching him hoard stuff for months now. I thought it was just the usual assortment of things he scavenges from round about, bits and pieces that no one wants any more. But you know what he's got hidden in there? Underwear.'

'What?'

'Bras. Camisoles and skimpy things.'

Dale struggles to make sense of it. 'Is that really so bad?' she says, asking herself as much as Beth.

'He's got them hanging off the ceiling, off the door handle. There's a pile of knickers in one corner and I don't know where he got them from. The other week he was escorted home by policewomen who caught him climbing over the back wall of one of those townhouses in Bank Street.'

Curiosity dulled with each detail, Dale goes through the motions of enquiring. 'Did he explain what he was doing?'

'No. He doesn't talk. He won't talk.'

'I guess that's not so unusual for him.'

'This is different. It's like . . . like he's floating away. And it doesn't matter what I do, there's no way I can reach him.'

Beth weeps, and Dale holds her tightly, petrified by the turbulence indoors, sheltering from the storm.

JANET SLIPS ANOTHER tiny white tablet under the blade of a knife and halves it. Harry swallows two doses of medication daily, one with breakfast and another at recess. She can't detect any difference in him but Miss Dobbin swears there's been a slight improvement, as if this measly gain justifies doping her son. Janet feels like a dealer, concealing the drugs inside marshmallow, her fingers sticky. Fooling who? It's a masking game.

She pops a pink marshmallow into her mouth, the powdery hide dissolving on her tongue. Cassie's favourite sweet. The two girls used to toast marshmallows over a winter bonfire. Cassie would jab hers into the flames, impaled on the end of a stick, in too great a hurry for her treat. The sugar would melt, blacken, blister then plop sizzling into the fire. She'd howl, demanding another and another, until Janet would be called to help her sister hold her stick steady above the heat.

Maybe the wonder drug would have turned Cassie into

the kind of girl who's easier to love: not too greedy, or too careless, or too hasty. Janet's head crackles as she argues with herself endlessly. One moment she is furious for bowing to those who favour medication – the teacher, the doctors, Nick. The next, she subdues her revulsion, willing to do whatever it takes to help her son. They tell Harry that the tablets are like wearing a pair of glasses – they'll help him to focus on the blackboard. No harm in a trial, she'd agreed; if she had refused and the unravelling had advanced, she'd be damned. She went to the local pharmacy, prescription in hand, where the older woman in charge arched her thin pencilled eybrows.

'We're seeing so many of these.' The woman sighed, with an inflection that massaged Janet's doubts. 'Mostly for boys. I've seen a lot of the teenagers who take these drugs end up on antidepressants.'

At last, a recruit for the resistance. One hundred or so dollars lighter, Janet left the shop with anecdotal fuel for her fears and a bag of natural remedies – pinebark, fish oil and a vitamin for calming very active children. Fired up, she raced home and flicked the computer on, reading up on diet, heartened by the idea of finding a culprit in food. Nick had blanched when she met him at the door that night, flushed with testimonials from parents who swore their changelings were tamed.

'Where are the clinical studies?' he enquired reasonably,

slinging his jacket over the back of the couch. Both children were in bed asleep.

'You don't think the pharmaceutical companies are going to fund research into alternative therapies, do you?'

Nick shook his head, as if he was too weary for rebuttal.

'Why are you so captive to science?' Janet pleaded. She knew how he raged with his colleagues at the rise of online experts – as if an afternoon cruising the net beat years of medical training. 'Why are you so closed to the possibility that there could be another way? How can you be so certain?'

'I'm not certain. I'm just saying there are quacks out there, okay?'

She wouldn't let up. 'There are success stories, too. Remember the doctor I told you about, the one who works with a dietician?'

Nick's eyes darkened. 'I cannot believe you are doing this to me.'

'I thought this was about Harry.'

'We have agonised for months now.' He spat the words at her. 'We consulted people we should trust. We got second and third opinions. We've been told that medication will help him learn, help him succeed, so he can see himself as someone who can complete tasks and win respect instead of being the class clown.'

He headed for the kitchen, reaching for a beer in the fridge.

Janet followed, fighting the urge to trip him, shake him, anything to dislodge his resolve.

'Listen to the side effects.' She grabbed the manufacturer's consumer guide, printed in text smaller than her old school Bible. 'Nausea, loss of appetite, impaired growth, headaches, mood changes, hair loss, confusion or hallucination. Seeing things that aren't there. Uncontrollable twitching, shortness of breath.'

Nick took the leaflet from her hands. 'Possible side effects. Possible,' he repeated. 'And we'll be watching for them closely. This is a trial, remember. It's not a life sentence. And so far the feedback's been positive.'

'Moderately positive,' she struck back. 'All Miss Dobbin wants is an easy life. She has our son for one year and she gets to call the shots. Then she's off. Adios.'

Nick got up close, his voice quiet. 'We made a decision. We have agreed to review it in two months.'

Janet opened her mouth to speak but he snookered her. 'I know this is hard for you. But guess what, it's hard for me, too. Not that you even stop to think about that. You're too busy chopping and changing, too busy drowning in panic. You don't care what you put us all through.' He knew he'd smacked the air straight out of her with this. And he lunged again. 'You're just like Harry. Maybe we should put you on the medication, too. What do you think?'

The Unexpected Elements of Love

She didn't punch him this time, although she wanted to hurt him. She fled from the house, winding up beside the harbour, where she sat on a rocky ledge as the tide sucked gently in and out and brooded on this shadow of disability lengthening over her family. Her parents had come undone managing Cassie. Wasn't it always the way? An easy child confirmed a coupling; a difficult child tested every premise of the partnership.

She returned to her slumbering household a few hours before the sun rose on yet another summery mid-winter morning.

Her surrender was not complete. She took Harry in for tests of hair, urine, blood. She collected bowel samples to be couriered to a lab. She put him on an organic, gluten-free diet, no dairy. She took delivery of drops and powders to be given three, four, five times a day. Harry refused to take the stuff in the brown glass bottles. He spat it out. The more she tried to help him, the more he resented her. So she stopped. And the mineral supplements that allegedly compensated for deficiencies were pushed further back into the pantry.

Maybe Nick is right. Maybe she can't stick to anything. Her disorganisation, her high energy – traits she once regarded as the harmless by-products of her busy existence, characteristics that once appealed to Nick – are polluting their marriage. Woken by Harry's nightmares, she goes to his bed, or he creeps into their warmth and stays put, denying Nick the sex he craves, adding another toxin to the mix.

Today's her morning off. Canteen duty and a pap smear. Whoopee! Whatever happened to facials and manicures? The clothes dryer beeps to signal the end of its cycle and she folds the clothes into warm piles. Two yellow plastic discs fall out of Harry's jeans pocket, ammunition from the space gun Aunt Cassie gave him last birthday. Cassie always gave the wildest presents, untroubled by a parent's antenna for danger, mess or noise. Harry had yodelled with excitement yesterday when Janet handed him a postcard addressed to him, all the way from a place called Mindil Beach, in Darwin.

> Hey Mr Blue Skies, I'm having the best time in the tropics. I found some cool stuff on the beach today that I'll show you next time we catch up. Think I might stay here for a while, that's if I don't go runny in the heat. Why don't you pester Mum to come up for a visit? Love to see you. Love to all.
> Aunty C.

Badgering is Harry's specialty; he started immediately. The 'maybe' Janet threw at him was merely a distraction while she arranged things.

She wants to see her sister, and to escape the heaviness that drapes her and Nick night after night. She can do some work while they're away. She's been corresponding via email with Felix Blake for weeks now, a storm chaser who runs an adventure tour business in Darwin, which she's learnt is the lightning epicentre of the world. Thrillseekers and nature worshippers pay Felix to take them into the wild for dress circle views of the Top End weather, always spectacular once the wet season begins. Janet is fascinated by these people's desire to brush up against the beasts of foul weather, and Felix Blake's novelty tourism could be the hook that she needs for a story, a tailor-made excuse for their escapade.

Just time before she rushes off to the canteen to log on to an airline website. She's distracted by a breaking news bubble reporting on a typhoon – fifty-six Filipinos, rag pickers, feared dead after heavy rains loosened the hillside above a rubbish dump outside Manila. She taps into a wire service and finds a two-par account of the disaster. Even white trash from a West Virginia trailer park would cultivate more column inches. World news services paid dearly for footage of the two-year-old boy sucked from his highchair by a twister in Oklahoma and dropped, in one piece, a kilometre away from what used to be his mother's kitchen. She assumes there will be no pictures of the rag pickers. Third World calamity usually doesn't interest the West, unless its own citizens are harmed. She's not proud of the brief sadness she spares the victims, either. But countries are like families – we look out for our own. Hopping on to the airline site, she books two return tickets to Darwin.

IT WAS ROY who suggested a walk. 'Not far,' he promised. 'Just up to the corner and back again.'

Beth is exhausted after a day sheltering indoors, blinds and curtains drawn, denying quarter to the sun, which has slipped summer's moorings. She feels like she's fighting a war with this heat; she has to be up early and conniving to outsmart its warmth before day breaks. But perhaps, she thinks, this will be the time to do what she's been putting off forever. 'What a grand idea,' she fibs.

She had set her trap in obvious spots, first on the arm of his chair, then on the kitchen table, then beside the bed, in the hope that he might glance at the newspaper article. Might pick it up, read it, and at last open up to her. The story has galvanised argument across the country. On the radio chat shows that tune her in to the outside world, everyone's got a view of the 54-year-old painter, beset by dementia, who elected to die one afternoon inside a stationwagon parked beside the ocean that sang her goodbye. The woman decided to end her life while she could still make sense of her predicament. She drew up her plan, procured the drugs, rented a bomb of a car and organised pets and papers, all of which surprised friends, who regarded her as reliably inefficient.

In the midst of this uproar, collared by microphones outside his surgery, is the doctor who'd introduced himself as a fellow stirrer way back when Roy was still high on the joy of his commission and Beth still had energy to spare for climbing up on a soapbox. Spokesman for the Voluntary Euthanasia Society, Dr Robert Kinane, refuses to deny or confirm any part in the woman's peaceful death but is not so reticent in fanning debate over her post-mortem. Beth had hoped the clipping would lead Roy beyond the particulars of the painter's choice and on to a closer understanding of his own, but it seems the story has passed him by.

Levering herself out of the armchair with Roy's help, Beth grips Cuz and they head out, leaving the front door ajar. Sounds carry in the warm, still air of the street. Windows and doors swing wide and neighbours move out on to balconies and rooftops, crawling forth from shady places, commiserating over common discomfort.

'Do you remember the doctor who wrote after I made a fuss at the coffee shop?' Beth asks, heart suddenly beating too swiftly. But at least she has made the first, tentative step.

Roy shrugs, which could mean that he doesn't remember,

or that his attention has wandered.

'Well, he's coming to Sydney next week for a public forum on death and dying.'

'Count me out. I'm not ready for death.' His voice is loud, jovial, and she hushes him as they nod at the old neighbour in singlet and tartan slippers, beagle in tow.

'I'm not ready either,' she says. 'But I'm thinking of going to see him.' This much is true. That she will be an audience of one is a detail she keeps to herself. 'I heard him on the radio today.'

'Sounds like a lone wolf to me.' Roy is staring with hungry eyes at a neighbour's skip that brims with rubbish.

'You've got to admire him for taking on the church and right-to-life groups. He only does what people ask of him. And what's wrong with wanting to escape the pain and loneliness of holding on?' Beth cannot believe her voice sounds so normal, as if they are chatting about the weather.

'Everyone always wants to take the short cut.' His downcast glance is code for 'let me be'. He pokes a crack in the footpath with his sandalled toe.

'If something happened to me, an accident or a stroke,' Beth starts, avoiding too many whys and wherefores, 'if I was lost to you, what would you do?'

'I would find you,' he says. 'The way you smell, our jokes, the children. You would never be lost to me.'

He misunderstands her so extravagantly, she has no heart

to continue. Then she remembers the compliment that Dale once paid her, 'You're a hard woman, Mum.'

'But what if you couldn't remember who I was? What if you couldn't remember my smell? What if you couldn't remember my jokes? What then?'

'If I couldn't remember you, then our lives would be over.'

Beth searches his gaze. Is he giving her permission?

They pause at the top of their street and she notices a light on in the cottage owned by their oldest neighbour, four years short of her century. She asks Roy to go and check on the grande dame. 'It'll only take a minute.'

Tired of her errands, he hesitates, and then the light is snuffed out. They turn back to walk home and he lobs Beth's question back to her.

'What would you do with me?' His voice is light.

'At the first sign of dribbling from either end, you're gone,' she says. But when she looks for his answering smile, his face is boarded over.

'Would that make it easier on you, packing me away?'

'Of course not. What would you want me to do?'

'Bury me in an old shoebox at the bottom of the garden,' he says, 'behind the shed.

'That's my spot,' she would once have kidded him. Not tonight. Now they inhabit a place inhospitable to the wryness of their past.

IN THE PRE-DAWN darkness, Nick loads their cases into the boot of the cab. He hands Harry his red backpack, loving the way Janet pulls him towards her for a hug, tight and close.

'Look after Mel,' is all she says. Father and daughter are leaving in the afternoon for a school camp on an island in the Hawkesbury River. 'Don't forget the tent. And the mozzie coils. They're in the laundry cupboard.'

They're mindful of each other. An unspoken truce.

'Good luck with Cassie,' he shouts, too late. He waves them off and jogs along the street until shortness of breath pulls him up at the crest of the first steep hill. The prospect of Harry, Janet and her sister together so far north niggles at him. As he runs, he looks for omens, which he finds in Darwin's history: the hardy frontier town has endured bombing and a cyclone. Some marriages survive equivalent mishaps, he tells himself, while others collapse at the first puff of misfortune.

The taxi driver ferries Janet and Harry to the airport as

the sky's coppery tint heralds the sun's advance; city-bound commuters cross paths with barflies and night owls bound for bed. Harry opens his backpack and discovers the bag of liquorice Nick tucked in there. He eats it immediately, blackening his teeth. Next he comes across a small package containing a waterproof watch with the face of a smiling sun. Janet helps secure the plastic band on his thin wrist, wondering how long it will take for the present to be lost.

Peak hour is almost over in the domestic terminal, the business folk already en route. In the gate lounge, passengers are colourfully dressed, unwinding for the leisurely tempo of a tropical outpost.

'I like the landings best,' Harry whispers to her as the plane taxis. He grips the seat, eyes scrunched tight as the wheels lift off the runway. Airborne, he relaxes, entertaining himself with the in-flight programs while Janet checks again that she's put Cassie's final postcard in her bag. On the front is a photograph of a stuffed crocodile called Sweetheart, seven hundred and eighty kilograms of snarl now behind glass in the Darwin museum. On the back is her sister's address, 21A Seymour Court. No mention of a suburb or a telephone number. The 'A' suggests a piggyback of a place, the broom cupboard of a duplex rented out on a week-by-week arrangement that accommodates Cassie's transience. Janet has sent news of their arrival on a postcard of her own.

She flips open a manila folder of literature on Darwin's thunderstorms. Their visit coincides with the build-up to the Wet, when the humidity reaches its zenith and residents find themselves longing for the cool of drenching rain. Felix Blake has warned her that she is weeks shy of seeing the pyrotechnics of thunder and lightning – news that Harry welcomed with clapping hands, although Harvey had to be convinced that the trip was still worthwhile. But he owed her one for showing up in the storm, and could hardly refuse the royal flush of images she'd waved so temptingly. He'd been practising golf shots with a putter kept in his office, but actually put it down to help her brainstorm titles.

'"Dr Dare" I like. But I don't want a science documentary about lightning, I'm telling you now.'

'Don't worry,' Janet soothed. 'This is about storm-chasers. What is it that drives them to chase crazy weather?'

'This Blake chap, he hasn't been struck by lightning, has he?' Harvey asked hopefully.

Janet shook her head. 'But he knows several people who have been hit, including one guy who was wearing a metal belt buckle that melted into his skin.'

'That's more like it. If you can get him on camera and wrangle storm footage out of him, the story might work.'

Janet thanked him but he'd already picked up his putter again, lining up an invisible tee.

The Unexpected Elements of Love

Harry's blanket slips to the floor and Janet pops it back in his pack. Bored with the movie and radio channels, he throws his juggling ball against the seat in front. Bounce, bounce, bounce, bounce. The last ball left from a pack of three. Learning the art of keeping three spheres in the air also means keeping track of them on the ground, a trick Harry is still learning.

Janet folds her arms around herself and shuts out the noise with earphones. She leans her seat back as far as it will go. For the next three days she will be the kind of mother who lets life slide. A goal that sounds to her like a dream.

DALE IS SORTING through boxes of memorabilia when she comes across the photograph of the two of them taken in their last year of school. Janet is laughing. Her thick black hair escapes from her high ponytail and she has a red hibiscus flower tucked behind an ear. No blazer; she was always losing it. Her socks are down around her ankles and she's wearing gym shoes. Dale, a prefect even after the last bell, smiles with her lips together, suppressing a giggle; two thin hazelnut-coloured plaits, boater on, blazer buttoned. The two of them look so soft and unlined. She still thinks of herself this way, or she did before moving back into her old room, the single bed a curt reminder of her life's narrowing.

She digs further into the box until she finds an airmail envelope postmarked with Her Majesty's profile. Inside is thin paper lined with Emil Bonner's confidences.

The Unexpected Elements of Love

Dear Dale

Oxford has frozen over so I am wearing the scarf and gloves you gave me, though the gloves make writing a tad cumbersome! The heater in my room is no match for the minus degrees of this miserable winter.

I miss you.

There are couples everywhere. I even had to step over a pair in the stacks of the college library yesterday. You, meanwhile, have probably not given me a moment's thought . . . ?

I'm slowly getting acclimatised: expectations bang into reality. You rub your head, put ice on the bump, and begin adjusting. It's a rather peculiar business. Love you to the nth degree.

Emil

Dale smiles at his proper turn of phrase. No wonder he fitted in over there so well.

She didn't cry back then, and she doesn't now. The only difference is that all those years ago, she was so sure love would come again. The photograph tucked inside the envelope shows a prankish, gangly boy. The purple scarf she gave him is wrapped like a turban around his head. Done with self-pity, she folds the letter and returns the envelope to the box, wondering whether Emil ever delves into his past to remember her. Odds are he's not living with his parents.

She's happy to be here. Of course she is. But there's

something so surreal about parenting her parents. She's managed to skip all together the stage of practising on her own brood, with the exception of her two cats, who mewed crossly all the way over in the car, the oldest disgracing herself upon arrival by peeing on the Persian runner in the hall. But there are bright moments, too. Yesterday's excavation had uncovered picture books from her childhood, favourite stories, one streaked with the scribble that had earned Billy a spank. Beth had held on to the books, perhaps for her grandchildren. Hope, like laughter, she had reminded Dale the other day, is the breath of life.

Dale fills her lungs with it, then returns to the household undergrowth that she must clear: garage sale, Billy's place, National Library, charity bin, dump. Everything has a place. Hers is to restore order.

'Tea?' The rasp of her father's voice precedes him.

'That'd be lovely, Dad,' she says, trying all over again not to be thrown by how he has shrunk. How he is disappearing before their eyes.

'When are you off?' he asks with a bright smile.

On Saturday he'd asked her this twenty times. She counted; counting soothes her irritability. Beth keeps a tally, too. It's a kind of game that keeps them from snapping at Roy, a man who rarely let his own impatience scald either of them. Dale does not reveal how she curbs her irritation at Beth, dipping into the stash of dope acquired for her by Billy.

She hears her mother stirring in the next room, the creaking of the bed and the shuffle of recalcitrant limbs as Beth pushes her frame to the door. Housebound now, her mother no longer goes to her exercise class. She begs off walking, and because Dale has moved back home she does not make the weekly excursion for coffee. She says she doesn't have the energy for the hurly-burly but Dale knows how this self-imposed exile irks her. The waiter has finally won. It's the dependency that needles Dale, and scares her. Not that Beth isn't spiky at times, which is why Billy has been called home to help.

Dale needs the power of numbers to steer Beth towards a plan for both her and Roy. As if tainted by his debilitation, her mother practises avoidance. Yesterday, the Canberra architects rang for Roy. Beth said he was in the studio, up to his armpits in toxic resin moulds, and could not take calls. She finessed the truth without compunction, protecting Roy to the end.

'I know he's getting close to finishing the sculpture. He gets very secretive, very withdrawn, very temperamental when the end's near . . . No, I know that . . . I'll ask him tonight when he comes in for a meal and get him to ring you tomorrow morning . . . Yes, he does. I'll tell him. 'Bye.'

Roy was in the studio, no dishonesty on that score. He spends six or seven hours out there each day, breaking only for the walk he takes at dusk, returning with satchel bulging and intense satisfaction in the set of his mouth.

Beth has not revealed to anyone how panic catches at her since the night of the storm. She frisks him with her eyes, searching for signs of the thickening of purpose that would once have howled down her doubt at his strange ways. Its absence fuels her dread. She hasn't even confided in Mora. Canberra is a small town. One indiscreet slip and rumour will spread. What counts is Roy's dignity.

Like a child plucking daisy petals, Beth oscillates. He'll hold together. He'll fall apart. He'll hold together. He'll fall apart.

Dale meets her mother in the hallway. Beth seems brighter this morning as she pushes her frame through the door.

'Out of my way,' she jokes. 'I'm in training for the hundred-metre sprint.'

Dale laughs and gives her a hug. 'That's more like you.'

'I'm sorry, sweetheart. The old gagbag almost ran out of puff.'

'I knew there was a second wind in store.' Dale stands back to let her pass. 'Would you like to come with me to the fish market and help me choose tonight's dinner?'

Beth frowns. 'I was hoping you could take your father to Freshwater Beach. He has a meeting there this morning with Max Waring.'

'A doctor?'

'No, a glassmaker. He's going to help Dad finish the sculpture.'

The Unexpected Elements of Love

Dale follows her into the kitchen and puts the kettle on before being asked. 'Why don't you come with us? You and I could have a coffee and watch for whales.'

But Beth shakes her head, as if she has other miracles to entertain her. 'I have an appointment down the street.'

Dale lets her mother's mystery be. Glad for the sign of a green shoot, she does not disturb its growth.

THE PLANE TREES shading the sculpture garden in the harbour-side park where Beth waits for Dr Kinane are so brittle that their leaves rasp in the breeze. The buffalo grass beneath her feet is like raffia matting. She smells death. Perhaps the trees have been poisoned by the owner of an apartment who would kill for a view of water daubed with yachts and ferries.

The whole park needs a spruce-up. Ten years ago she would have bent down and binned the rubbish. Foil wrappers, plastic bags and drink cans dirty the path leading to the cluster of five free-standing sculptures cast in bronze. The sixth piece, set a little apart, is her husband's whimsy, built from round, smooth river stones to make a cairn that tilts slightly, as if blown off centre by the winds that whip through here on wild days.

The council's urban planners commissioned the sculptures to counter criticism of shrinking public space. But the park rarely attracts art lovers or loiterers of benign intent. Instead, dogs cock a leg on Roy's sculpture; no four-legged animal can pass by without squirting a claim. Roy didn't mind, pointing out that the stones were made to weather a trickle or a torrent.

Joggers pound past Beth, eyes glazed and ears plugged into music or talk. Rubber soles scuff the pavement and she catches a drip of sweat flicked from a wet brow. Brandnames stripe their chests, along with the brag of triathlons and ocean swims from here to there and back again. She's intrigued by the speed and agility of well-tuned bodies, everything in perfect mechanical order. They could be dancing for the rapture in her face as she drinks in their perfection. Not one of them gives her a second look.

She feels her transparency acutely now. The X-ray stares. People look through her body and her opinions, eyes wandering off to light upon younger faces. But Dr Kinane's her age. Two grey ghosts, no one will notice them. Even so, her desire for discretion breeds intestinal butterflies.

Since they began corresponding, she has read both his books. She knows the story of his wife, who persuaded him that the only way she could beat lymphoma was to take control of what little was left of her life. She was being treated by a friend, who administered the fatal dose of morphine without fuss or hand-wringing on a day of their choosing. That was twenty-five years ago. Life, while no less precious, was more of a gamble back then; it was a time when accidents happened without the bark of liability forever chasing blame.

Dr Kinane has not shied from telling Beth the full cost of his complicity. His son, a boy when his mother died, has grown intolerant of his father's philosophy, believing that God's will was gazumped. Beth wonders if Dale might agree with him. She knows Billy will adjust, whatever happens.

A man approaches and she recognises Kinane from the photograph inside his dust jackets. He stands heads taller than she had imagined, and looks younger, she thinks, eyeing the sharp crease in his grey pants, the tightness of his black leather belt and a smile too white for seventy-four years of use.

Beth in the flesh is not quite what he'd expected, either. He sees how her walking frame could trip a person up with the impression of fragility. Not beautiful, although she was once, before her nut-brown skin crumpled.

Apologetic for making Beth wait in the heat, he sinks down beside her on the slatted wooden bench. They begin with the warm spring weather. 'I'm overdressed,' he says, removing his blazer. 'And I've been running from meeting to meeting, trying to do too much in less than no time.'

Pleasantries over, they get down to business. Kinane calmly draws Beth out on her purpose. What exactly does she want to discuss today?

Their exchange is stilted. Beth struggles with notions so despicable, she tries to sterilise their delivery, couching her request in language laundered of intent, as if she is requesting aspirin to cure an ache.

'I want to purchase two doses of the drug. I don't know if we'll ever use it, but I want the choice. Just in case.'

'So as to help your husband?'

She nods. Yes, so as to help Roy.

'And this is what he wants? I mean, you've talked about it?'

'He's close to finishing his sculpture. I can't distract him. But even so, I know exactly how he feels. We've talked about it so many times, how we don't want to keep going when it gets too hard.' She touches Kinane's hand, pleading. 'Please, I need to know that I can rescue him. If I have to.'

Kinane appreciates Beth's directness, but her speaking for her husband makes him reticent. 'I can put you in touch with a Sydney doctor, a geriatrician who you and Roy should go and see together.' He writes the name and number on one of his cards and hands it to her.

Beth stares at him, suddenly and absurdly close to tears. Somehow she had expected more from this meeting. As if Kinane could sweep into their lives and orchestrate their exit. Lessen the unbearable burden of making this decision.

'This geriatrician, is he sympathetic?'

Kinane doesn't give anything away. He has sound legal reasons for his professional detachment, as well as serious financial limits. 'I'm sure he'll do what he can.'

A belt of wind gusts through the reserve. Beth wonders whether Roy has sent it in silent protest.

Kinane's phone rings and he excuses himself, pacing out of her earshot, talking volubly.

Beth watches him; she is attracted to him, and revolted. He's an insider in a black market, the only person she knows who can broker the connection she so desperately needs, the fallback, the escape plan for a calm departure, should they see fit. The element of 'maybe' soothes her complicity, but barely.

Is this so different, she wonders, from her decision to terminate a pregnancy conceived in the muddle of menopause, just as arthritis struck? Her initial relief that the barest beginnings of life could be scrubbed out was overtaken, later, by remorse. Every time she meets someone who is roughly the same age as her unborn child, she mourns afresh.

The message 'we are in this world to make life easier for other people' had been embroidered and framed on the surgery wall. One life saved, another spent. Something about Dr Kinane's manner, or perhaps her own ethical suppleness, makes her queasy.

A jogger, dripping in singlet and shorts, pauses at the

entrance to the park and checks his watch. He sits on the grass and flops backwards, looking up at the sky through the filigreed leaves of a jacaranda. His hairy legs splay open and Beth turns away from the unedifying sight of crotch. She hears an electronic purr and a white-haired lady wearing wrap-around dark glasses whizzes by on a scooter.

The doctor is deep in conversation, his bottom propped disrespectfully on the stone lip of Roy's sculpture. He catches Beth's eye and mimics with his hand the jabbering jaw in his ear. Almost on cue the cicadas start, slowly at first, but within seconds they are screaming. The jogger rolls on to his elbows in wonderment as Beth cups her hands over her ears.

Dr Kinane pockets his phone and walks towards her, seeming to shrink from their warning cry.

OVER THE SOUTH Alligator River, Harry goes to the bathroom for the umpteenth time, squeezing past the gentleman on the aisle who has been engrossed in a mathematical textbook for the entire journey. Far below, the river's meandering loops tattoo the earth.

Inside the terminal, Janet finds the hire-car counter where she queues while Harry hops on a luggage trolley, picking up speed, shaving past passengers, turning the head of a heavyweight security guard who seems teased by this puzzle of a boy in orbit.

Outside, the sound of crickets thickens the humidity and Harry whimpers, 'I'm hot. Hot and thirsty. I need a drink.'

'Wait until we get to the hotel,' she begs, determined to press ahead. They find the car, which is spanking clean.

'It stinks in here,' he grizzles.

'After a few days of us, it'll ripen up.' She has an idea. 'You read the map, okay? Be the navigator and lead us into town.'

He tears it up. Shreds the pages on to the floor of the car and screams for the drink.

'The hotel has a swimming pool,' she offers. But this promise is old news. She pulls into a ten-pump service station on the outskirts of the airport to arm themselves for the drive to Cassie's place. Harry sucks contentedly on his can while Janet locates the street in the directory, thankful that there is only one Seymour Court in Darwin.

For years Cassie has hidden her whereabouts, appearing suddenly on birthdays or on Christmas Eve, laden with presents, overly generous. In between their hugs and thank-yous, they pushed away the question of how she'd come by the cash to pay for the gifts. On Boxing Day she'd vanish, calling next from a pay phone or sending a postcard. Janet learned to accept these irregular missives as routine but their mother could never let go of the fear that her youngest daughter might one day disappear for good.

Numbers 21 and 21A stud the same gatepost. The house sits back from the road, barely visible amidst the mirror bushes, palms and frangipani trees. Swathes of orange bougainvillea have leapt the neighbour's fence to shake papery blooms over the lawn. The front door is open and bamboo blinds tap against the windows – breezes and lizards have right-of-way in a town where the outside has a habit of barging in. Observing this protocol Harry scoots inside, ears pricked to the giggles and shouts coming from the back garden. Janet follows him through the cool wooden interior, glancing into a kitchen where Tibetan prayer flags flutter over the vivid finger paintings, photos, posters and newsletters tacked on to walls and the fridge.

'Cassie?' Harry shouts from the back step, staring down into an unruly garden that slopes towards a garage at the rear of the property, where Janet suspects her sister dwells.

Curiosity lures a dark-skinned little girl with short black hair from her hiding spot. She wears a grown-up's sandals on her wee feet and a string of fake pearls swings from her scrawny neck.

'Gotcha!' Cassie pounces into view, plumper than Janet remembers, a faded batik sarong tied over a one-piece swimming costume. She slides her large feet into the reclaimed scuffs and bounds up the back steps, clasping Janet and then Harry in her warm, sweaty arms.

'What have you done to your hair?' Janet mourns, running her fingers through Cassie's thick dark stubble.

'I've gone native. It's too hot and I can't be bothered with hair. I've even shaved my pubes,' she announces, pleased to inflict a mild shock.

A hand tugs on Janet's hem, and she glances down to see the little girl grinning up at her.

Cassie does the introductions. 'This is Grace. She lives here with her mother, Annie, who's at work. So I'm the boss.'

Janet smiles. 'For a moment, I thought she might be yours. That you'd kept her hidden from us all these years.'

Cassie clasps her sister's shoulders. 'I cannot believe you just said that!'

Janet begs forgiveness. 'It was just a joke, Cass.'

'Uh-uh, no way. You can sense it.'

'Sense what?' Janet's nerves prickle.

'I'm pregnant.' She takes Janet's hands in hers, holding on too tight. 'Isn't that wild? The best thing you've ever heard?'

'Oh, Cassie.' Janet covers her fumbling with a clumsy embrace. Inside, their mother's voice wells up. How could Cassie have been so careless? How on earth will she manage? 'How many months are you?'

'Three and a half.'

Apalled at herself, Janet calculates if there is still time for a change of heart. 'Who's the dad?'

'A guy. Obviously.' She laughs, throwing Janet the old 'der' look of their childhood. 'But he doesn't know about it. And don't ask me where he is, because I seriously haven't got a clue.'

'You don't think your child will want to know?'

Blocked by Janet's logic, Cassie turns abruptly to other practicalities, because here at least she has done the sums. 'I'm going to mind Grace for Annie, to pay the rent. I mean, I have to hang around here for the baby anyway.'

Stunned into silence, Janet follows Cassie to sit at a cane table with wonky legs. Cassie takes a pinch of tobacco from a beaded pouch and rolls herself a thin cigarette. She takes a long, satisfying drag, and catches the censure in Janet's eyes. 'I have a couple a day, okay? Is that such a crime?'

'I guess not.' Janet reaches for the pouch. 'Mind if I have one?'

'Be my guest.'

The champagne Janet's brought along in her bag is warm. Cassie fetches two plastic tumblers, pouring a thumbnail's worth of bubbly for herself. They talk about Annie, who is separated from Grace's father and is grateful, according to Cassie, for the childcare arrangement she and Cassie have nutted out.

'Come and I'll show you my place,' says Cassie, and they weave through the greenery to a converted garage furnished frugally – single bed, sink, bar fridge, an electric kettle and a venetian blind that hangs askew across a small window. 'I use the bathroom in the house,' Cassie explains, before Janet can ask, 'and sometimes at night, if I'm busting, I just take a squirt outside in the garden.'

Her beachcombing gear hangs from a hook on the back of the door, like the overalls of a fireman ready for the call. Beside the bed are three watches, laid out carefully next to the framed photographs Janet gave her sister years ago. One is of

Harry and Mel, all teeth, and the other is of Cassie and Janet at the same age. Janet is looking at the camera while Cassie's head is thrown back as she clutches her doll by its hair; their mother's outstretched hands enter the frame, about to intervene. No sign of their father, an invisible man since the day he abandoned his brood, the same year Cassie started kindy.

Janet does not let herself ask how Cassie will cope with a baby in this shed. She lets her sister talk, unfolding long, wandering stories packed tight with jokes and intrigue, populated by nomads like Cassie herself is, or was. Janet's not sure how mothering might change a sister whose unpredictability is the one constant she has ever been able to depend on.

'Give me some time to get used to this, Cass.'

'I'm still getting used to it myself. Mum would have had a fit.' She picks their mother perfectly. They have both been bitten by her, differently.

Exhausted, Janet rounds up Harry, prying him from Grace's side, and they amble up to the car.

'I wish I had a little sister, Mum. Why can't I?' he pleads.

Cassie bends down and whispers something to him as they hug.

Janet opens the door and ushers Harry inside. She kisses Cassie on the cheek, surprised at the rush of emotions flooding her. At how protective she feels. 'Why don't you come with us to Kakadu tomorrow? We'll get back some time early afternoon.'

'Can I bring Grace?'

'Why not.'

They drive off, Harry waving madly at Grace until she is out of sight. At that exact moment he becomes insatiably hungry, ravenous, so that she has to search for a fast-food joint. When they stop at an all-night noodle bar she notices his dirty bare feet.

'Grace hid them,' he lies. 'She's a serial shoe thief.'

Janet laughs at his claim. 'By the way, what did Aunty Cassie say to you when we were leaving?'

'Just that she always wished she'd had a little sister too.'

CASSIE AND GRACE catch a bus the next morning, arriving at the hotel before breakfast with Harry's runners in a plastic bag. Cassie is dressed in her beachcombing gear, sporting long khaki pants from the army disposal store, jungle fatigues with zips securing the pockets down each leg. Here's where she stashes the trinkets her metal detector sniffs out when she takes to the shores at dusk, stealthy as game coming to drink at the waterhole's edge, arriving as the last of the crowd toss towels over shoulders and leave. Socks protect the skin peeping between the straps of her rubber sandals. Penguin feet, thinks Janet. The outfit's completed by a long-sleeved shirt buttoned at the wrist and her tan vest, padded with hiding places. The vest, the kind worn by foreign news crews, was a gift from Janet. Cassie loves it. Coins go in the money belt slung around her hips. Rings, if she's lucky, into the right leg pocket. Watches, the jackpot, are kept in the left. It's all lost property. Anyone's to claim.

The children play with breakfast, Harry eating only his yolks while Grace prefers their white greasy skirts. Cassie orders the lot, wiping her plate clean with Janet's leftover toast.

They're meeting Felix in the foyer. Peering through the atrium, Janet singles him out from the milling guests – a man somewhere in his fifties, hat pushed back on his head, his hiking boots, shorts and Yakka shirt comfortably rumpled, lived in. A phone in its jacket is hooked on to his plaited belt.

Felix is taking them to Kakadu to see rock paintings of lightning men, which Janet will film on minicam for the editor to drop into her segment. They drive out of town in his new silver four-wheel drive, which boasts a periscope for fording rivers and 'Thunderstorm Tours' in large black letters, front, back and sides. A jagged lightning fork hangs from his rear-view mirror. Grace and Harry are wedged either side of Cassie in the back seat, along with Felix's miniature fox terrier, who does not complain at being wrapped in Harry's blanket and nursed vigorously before Grace demands a turn.

Clouds are building in the blue sky and Felix starts unfolding tales for Janet of all he's seen in his years of storm chasing. He lingers over the imagery – double-barrelled lightning, horizontal strikes. Nights illuminated by X-ray flashes that electrify the blackness. The scariest episodes he keeps for campfires. Even so, Janet sneaks an anxious glance back at Harry, hoping that his pulse isn't galloping into a panic, but he's preoccupied by chatter with Grace and Cassie.

Immense popcorn clouds offer the only motion along a road that you could rule a margin by. Cassie points out salmon-pink gum trees and Harry spots multi-storey termite nests, pinnacles punching through the low scrub. Janet had wondered if he'd be scared out here in this alien landscape, so far from the bumper-to-bumper steel and concrete of home. But he's got company to engage him.

Felix is also a suburban boy, from way back. For years he'd worked at the uranium mine up here, an outcast from his family who lived in a Melbourne suburb that proudly declared itself to be nuclear free. After three decades in a place he'd only ever planned on passing through, he still denies he belongs, which qualifies him as a true local. Unfortunately for Janet, he bears no resemblance to the Dr Dare that Harvey had hoped she'd capture. 'Severe thunderstorms outwit computer models,' he tells her earnestly. His facts are stacked like bricks, solid. 'Meteorologists can predict the conditions in which they develop and monitor them once they occur, but even so the buggers are complex to interpret.'

Janet tosses him questions and makes notes as she drifts in and out of his monologue, catching the chatter in the back seat.

Harry is asking Grace to name her very favourite things. 'I'm four,' she says. 'And I've got a Mum. Um.'

'No, no. What do you *like* best in the whole world?'

The littlest is struck dumb until Cassie whispers in her ear.

'The water slides at the pool!' she shrieks.

'My turn,' Cassie demands. 'What's the naughtiest thing you've ever done?' She snickers, then answers herself. 'Carving my full name into the side of Mum's car.'

Janet can think of much worse sins but she simply clucks, 'Don't put ideas into their heads.' This is a good day, or as Harry would say, a white cloud day. A day when a tipple of hope curls up from the toes. Away from the classroom, the office, the instructions, the "sit stills". A day of accepting that life is an hourly proposition and like the weather it can change in a snap.

Harry's started to listen in stereo, like Janet, switching from back seat to front, and as Felix launches into yet another graphic description of storm activity and chaos, he chews the collar of his shirt, one eye on the sky. 'How do you know when lightning is coming?' he asks, and before Janet can deflect him, Felix is away, flattered by the attention.

'Moments before it hits, there's a rumble and a rush of cold wind. But there are some wise elders around the place who hear lightning before it knocks.' Harry's eyes widen as Felix tells them a story about a government do he'd attended in Kakadu once, when one of the traditional owners had excused herself suddenly and sped off in her car moments before a massive explosion of thunder and lightning hit only metres from the marquee where guests were taking refreshments.

'But how did she know it was coming?' asks Harry, breathless with tension.

Cassie puts an arm around his shoulders and grins. ''Cause the blackfellas have got this thing about instincts, right? They listen to what's going on in here.' She taps Harry's heart. 'And not so much what's going on in here.' Now she taps his head.

Felix throws a wry grin over his shoulder. 'Or she just had to get somewhere in a hurry.'

Cassie rolls her eyes. 'Don't tell me, you're a science guy? Just dry, straight facts all the way?'

'I'm not saying that. I just don't like making mystery where there doesn't need to be any. And I'm telling you, plenty of blackfellas get sick of being treated like they're any different from the white mob.'

'But they are different. How can they not be?'

Felix just shrugs, not prepared to start a barney neither can win. 'Yeah, whatever.'

'Whatever,' mimics Grace. 'Whatever.'

As the car turns off the highway even the youngest of their party hushes, quietened by the grey and orange streaked cathedral of rock looming before them. Felix pulls into the car park, between a campervan and a mini-bus ready to depart as the last of its middle-aged passengers slams the door shut behind him.

'Hats,' commands Janet. The furry warmth clothes them in a film of sweat before a single step is taken.

'Gracie, be careful.' Harry bends down to lock eyes with his friend as he gives his instruction, just as Janet does when she warns him against shooting across the road without looking both ways or swinging his cricket bat through the air without first checking for kids likely to be caught in his arc. He takes Grace's hand tenderly, and the instant catches her unprepared, like the day she heard him laugh for the first time. He was barely three months old, lying on a blanket spread out on the lounge-room floor when Cassie had unexpectedly turned up and plonked herself down beside him to play.

Felix shuts the car door on the little dog, who goes by the name of Mortein, 'because she keeps the snakes at bay'. The terrier's face is forlorn as she realises that she won't be accompanying them. The path up into the rocky gallery is signposted in several languages. Janet falls into step with Felix as he crams her head with dates and theories about the people who painted their stories on the cave walls. She thinks of a theory she'd come across in her research, that boys like Harry were once chosen by elders to be scouts and trackers, highly prized for their ability to detect early warning of trouble.

Cassie and the children are impatient to reach the lookout at the top of the cliff and plead to go on ahead.

'Watch them like a hawk,' Janet tells her sister.

Cassie lifts her fleshy arms high, as if to fly. The children copy her, swooping behind.

Inside the cave Janet flicks on her minicam and records the paintings. Felix steers her toward his jewel, the lightning man who goes by the name Namarrgon. He's ringed by an electric charge; the hammers strung to his knees, head and elbows are for knocking thunderously together. She's surprised by an urge to reach out and touch him, to run her fingers over the rock and pigment.

They leave the dark coolness and duck back out into the dazzle of sun, taking the steps up to the lookout.

'Jesus!' Felix shouts from behind Janet and she looks up to see the children skipping on the ledge, beyond the metal safety barrier. Grace heeds the adults' warning calls and scrambles back, but Harry laughs and pushes a rock the size of a canteloupe over the lip of the cliff. The splintering crack of its descent ends in a distant thud down below.

Felix swears and pushes past Janet. He takes Harry by the scruff and all but shakes him. 'What the hell do you think you're doing?'

Janet grabs Grace and hollers for her sister.

'Over here,' Cassie finally answers.

When Janet sees her squatting on the ground, relief slams into fury.

Cassie ambles over with her hands a cage. 'Hey, check it

out. I've found this amazing orange cricket and . . .' She trails off as she takes in the adults' stormy faces. 'What's up?'

'I asked you to watch the kids. Did you forget?'

'No,' Cassie says warily. 'Why? They look okay to me.'

'They're not bloody okay,' Felix snaps. 'Harry's been playing funny buggers.'

Cassie's quick to the defence. 'Hey, leave him alone.'

'I didn't mean to . . .' tries Harry, tremulous as punishment threatens. He looks to Janet. 'Mum, tell him I didn't mean to.'

Felix gets in first. 'You realise you or Gracie could've fallen off and broken your necks? And what if someone got hit with that rock, what then?'

This horrible thought had not yet occurred to Janet.

Felix takes Harry's hand. 'Come on, mate. You and me are going to go check out where it landed and we can have a little talk about self-discipline on the way.'

Harry's horrified. He stares at his mother, pleading for her to get him off the hook. 'Mum? I don't want to go.'

But for once Janet is not coming to his aid. 'You'll be fine.' She nods at Felix, who leads a sullen Harry down the escarpment, his confidence in Harry's capacity to calculate risk unsullied by the experience of repetition.

Cassie is clutching Grace's hand, staring sulkily at her sister. 'Don't start, okay? I'm sorry I wasn't watching them, but it's all worked out fine.'

'Sorry doesn't cut it. And once you're a mother, you'll work that out for yourself.' Janet tries to stay cool, to reason. 'You're going to have a baby of your own, Cass. You've got to learn to be more careful. You need to stay three steps ahead.'

'And keep my kid on a leash, right? 'Cause that's worked so well with Harry. I mean, look how together he is.'

Grace startles at their raised voices. The sisters are back in the volatile country of their childhood, the place where Cassie could flip over an annoyance, a smell, Janet's chatter, a lost toy, provoking scenes that never ended in tears alone.

Janet nips at her sister. 'Like you know the first thing about loving anyone other than yourself.'

Cassie drops Grace's hand and is gone, heading towards the car park at a run.

'Is Harry in trouble?' asks Grace, and Janet hears Miss Dobbin in the sigh that precedes her explanation. By the time they reach the car park, Cassie is over the far side, disappearing into a battered campervan. 'Cassie? Wait,' Janet calls. But the driver is already accelerating, taking away her sister, who doesn't even shoot a backward look as the van picks up speed. 'That's right,' Janet roars at Cassie's smoke, 'run off and leave Grace behind. Is that how you're going to look after your own kid?'

Grace is crying now, and Janet opens the passenger door to sit her down. The little dog leaps out, full of joy at being freed.

Janet flops on to a bench and watches Grace, who finds a pair of Felix's boots and slips her feet inside. She's hilarious, matchstick legs barely able to lift her prize. Footsteps announce Harry's arrival; his curls are plastered to his forehead. No sign of his hat. He's subdued, shrugging off Grace when she tries to comfort him.

Felix arrives moments later. 'Who left the bloody door open?' he asks sharply.

'Me,' Janet owns.

'Dogs aren't allowed in national parks. I thought I explained that.' He whistles loudly for the dog, then casts Janet an accusing look. 'I'm not leaving here without her.' He wanders the car park calling her name. Janet trails him, willing Mortein to appear. Please don't let the dog be lost, she prays. It is Harry who hears the terrier scuffling behind the toilet block. Felix tips the dog into the car without a word. Disgraced, the lot of them, except for Grace, who's a quick study in the art of survival.

'Where's Cassie?' Felix asks, doing a head count.

'She's hitched a ride back,' Janet says casually.

Felix doesn't pry but Janet recognises censure in the brisk economy of their departure. She imagines his riff: if Harry was his kid – well, his kid wouldn't do such a thing. And if the boy did, he'd get all that he deserves. Janet can only hope that Felix recovers in time for the interview he's promised to give her tomorrow.

The Unexpected Elements of Love

They drive in silence. Only the dog wins Felix's pardon – she lies on her back, busking for a cuddle.

Janet feels a tap from behind and a scrunched piece of paper falls on to her lap. She smooths it open. 'Don't unlove me.'

'Not possible. Not ever. Never,' she writes back to the boy who once assured her cheerily that anything is.

BETH LEANS ON Cuz, turning to acknowledge the toot from Tas who's idling in next-door's driveway while he waits for Doreen to put her face on for a jaunt to the club. He tumbles out of the car and lumbers over to join her, tucking his shirt into his khaki shorts, always dressed, it seems to Beth, as if he might be called any minute to fix a burst sewerage pipe.

'I see your son's up,' he says, with a nod in the direction of Billy's old Volvo, parked carelessly wide of the curb. Tas's habit of stating what you already know has kept Beth and Roy amused for years. One or other would scuttle inside from their meetings over the fence or on the street to relay the latest baton of banality. 'Bit of rain' if it's wet, or 'nice day' if it's not. One day Roy stepped out wearing a tea cosy on his head, bidding his neighbour a cheery good morning. Tas played it straight down the middle.

'You've got a tea cosy on your head,' he said to Roy, who replied, 'Just keeping the pot warm.' Tas had loved that one.

The Unexpected Elements of Love

He will have the last laugh, Beth thinks.

There still remains a glimmer of the Roy who loves an eccentric prank but now he hides her clothes in odd places, trawling through cupboards while she and Dale sleep.

'How long's Bill here for?' Tas asks, lifting his terry towelling hat and running a hand through the oily grey strands underneath.

'Just the weekend. Dale's here, too. We're having a family summit,' she adds, instantly regretting the release of this much information. But Tas doesn't sieve sentences for meaning.

'We haven't seen much of you lately, but we've heard plenty of banging from the shed. Not that he's bothering us.' Tas grins. 'What's he building, a nuclear missile?'

It's a cracker of a joke for Tas, but Beth freezes at the mention of Roy's studio. Part of her clings to the possibility that he is creating something magnificent in there, but each day she becomes more certain that the studio conceals a hideous monument to her husband's disappearance.

Doreen appears at the front door and Tas tips his hat at Beth, who doesn't maintain the charade of promising to get together for drinks. Past that, she thinks, waving at Doreen, admiring the faux zebra-skin coat and large sunglasses cornered by gold medallions. Doreen still dyes her hair jet black, as fake as the animal hide around her shoulders. Beth wonders whether she, too, might have shaken her fist at oldness, if arthritis hadn't got to her first.

Tas toots again as they take off, leaving Beth to inspect the letterbox. Amongst the junkmail is an environmental newsletter addressed to Roy. She glances at the report of an oceanographer's trip to the poles, where the ice is thinning. She screws the magazine up and throws it away, so as not to hex Roy with hopelessness.

The nature strip is dust blown. She can remember the last heavy rain – the night her husband brought an oar home as proof of the weather's crazy turn. From inside she hears Billy's voice, singing a song she doesn't recognise.

When Dale suggested they call Billy home for a meeting, she agreed, spotting an opportunity to help the children prepare for Roy's departure with talk of homecare services and nursing homes, none of which she could ever contemplate. This is her secret. She has made an appointment with the physician recommended by Dr Kinane, who might help her map a more dignified exit from the maze of derangement. But she won't be taking Roy along.

She rests her weight on the walking frame and feels the heat of the sun on her back. Not far to go, she thinks.

THEY SIT AROUND the kitchen table, the empty chair at its head bearing witness to their treachery. Roy is in the studio. Billy takes notes with a sharpened pencil that skates along the lined page of his notebook. After listening to his mother's story, he sets out what he calls a 'care plan' with the coolness of a professional paid to counter every unseen hitch. Beth allows herself to play along. He wants his father assessed. He will take leave from his job and come home to help. He says there are drugs to slow the brain's decline. He asks Dale to describe their father's behaviour. He talks through his own observations of Roy. He gives them a list of questions designed to help families detect warning signs.

He talks so much that Beth drifts off, watching the wasps duck in and out of their nest in the eaves outside the window. She can tell her son is pleased at his newfound authority after years in Dale's shadow. His sister was always the high achiever while he grazed on the lower slopes, never confident of matching her abilities, let alone his father's. He tells Beth he'll invite a geriatrician friend of his over for dinner, to observe Roy. That's as far as the quislings get before Beth sidetracks them with a perusal of the questions to test cognitive functioning.

'I fall into most of these categories,' she says. '"Often misplaces things, notices a loss of incentive, has difficulty performing familiar tasks".'

Dale looks at her with a wan smile. 'Maybe, Mum. But you haven't brought an oar into the house.'

Beth shrugs. 'I'm not rowing against the tide.'

'Anyway, the oar is probably for Dad's sculpture,' Billy points out.

Beth honours his loyalty with a small smile. Dale excuses herself to take a shower and they sit silently, until Billy gets up and goes outside for a closer look at the wasp nest. He reaches for the strawbroom on the verandah and Beth realises what he is about to do. She shouts at him to stop, but he doesn't hear her. The wasps are her low-maintenance pets. They never bother her.

She can't get up quickly enough. Searching for something to throw against the window, she grabs a set of keys, hurling them at the glass as Billy strikes his target with a blow. The window shatters at the instant the nest explodes. Now homeless, the wasps take revenge.

That night the family attempts a game of Scrabble, Roy's

idea. Beth goes first, placing a J on a triple letter to make the word 'joyful', however inappropriate to the mood around the table. Roy goes next and the wait for him to choose a letter drags out forever. He doesn't lift a finger to compose his choice. No one wants to take control of his letters, as Beth used to do with the children thirty or more years ago. He had been harder on them, determined that they should learn to think for themselves.

They sit shuffling the ivory squares on their racks. After an excruciating interval, Roy selects his letters, one by one, and arranges them into a word. 'Stang'.

ROY'S CHAIR HAS lost a castor but there's no time to replace it as he drags himself to the finish. He makes lists of what he must accomplish. 'Wednesday', he writes, staring at the word until it slips nonsensically out of his grasp.

Twice now he has mangled his bearings only two blocks from the front door, thrown into disorientation in the time it takes traffic lights to change. He sat one day for hours on a bus stop bench before realising he was on a road he has known most of his life. Tas and Doreen were walking home from the club and swept him up good naturedly. Well over the legal limit, their handicap was confined to co-ordination of fine and gross motor skills, while Roy could open gates and fit keys into locks but was at sea making other connections.

He gets through these ordeals the same way you find your footing in pitch black. He listens for conversational cues, papering over glitches, doing all he can to hide his befuddlement. There is a sculpture garden nearby, where he and Beth sometimes sit, and there is a cairn of stones that he knows to be his work only because Beth says so and a plaque confirms it. The cairn leans to one side and he wants to straighten it up. Or knock it down.

But the sculpture he is now building makes him laugh. A giant dinghy, it will be cast in glass, with the help of Max Waring, a kindly man who's glad for the fun of Roy's fantasy after a lifetime manufacturing windows in a city smitten with construction. He has promised to steer Roy home, taking care of every last detail.

The dinghy will sit on a fluorescent glass puddle. The colours lurid: purple, red, orange, blue. A pink frog squats on yellow rocks, like a Disney animation. His friend Morris was goggle-eyed when Roy described the work to him over lunch at the faculty club.

'Mutation,' Roy said, stirring his coffee with a knife. 'It will gleam in that grey courtyard.'

He registered the shock in Morris's eyes at this unexpected lurch into kitsch. His friend could never understand that this is the upside to losing grip – the invisible strings controlling his impulses are twanging and snapping. There are hours when this noise deafens him and he curls up in his chair with his fingers in his ears, rocking, unable to work. And there are other times when exhilaration lifts him up and over the fog of dementia.

Max is frustrated some days as Roy prevaricates over

decisions, undoing them, trying a new configuration, abandoning it, then returning to the original plan. There is much fussing over the smallest of dimensions as they position the dinghy, adjusting its angle of repose, vascillating over just where the oar should sit. Roy refuses to replace the varnished wooden paddle with a glass replica, determined that it stand as a barometer exposed to the weather. After three attempts to persuade him otherwise, Max bowed to the sculptor's stubbornness, salvaging the collaboration. He allows Roy the benefit of artistic temperament to cover all manner of extremes. They take walks along the beach to reboot him when his reasoning scatters.

Max suspects the sculpture's unveiling will cause a sensation beyond the tight circle of Australia's art scene. Its lollipop hues resemble nothing he has ever seen in a public space, and there is something shocking in Roy's lurid poke at a world unconcerned by the altering of the seasons. On this last point, Roy's sobering pessimism has infected him.

Next week the glass puddle will be cast. Max had phoned Roy yesterday to brief him on a minor hitch. The sculpture, he said, had almost been bumped from the factory's schedule by a Saudi sheik who wanted glass icebergs for his polar bear enclosure.

'Very funny,' Roy said dryly.

'I'm not joking.'

NOBODY ANSWERS JANET'S frantic knock at 21A. She peers through the window, calling her sister's name. Harry and Grace are flaked out in the back seat of the car. Felix dropped them off at the hotel an hour ago. If he thought 'good riddance', he didn't show it, mindful perhaps of the publicity Janet might deliver him.

All she wants to do is find her sister. Should they wait here? Should they go back to the hotel? She thinks of Mindil Beach, of the postcard Cassie sent to Harry. She consults the directory and decides it's as good a start as any.

The children stir as she pulls into the parking bay, just ahead of a double-decked coach bringing tourists to see the sunset, tonight masked by clouds. Felix's tours are bedevilled by the same variable.

On the beach Janet scans the people circling picnic rugs and slumped in canvas chairs, looking for a loner in their midst. Harry is the first to shout as Janet sees her sister's metal proboscis gliding along the curved shoreline. He runs to greet her, Grace at his heels. Janet almost throws her watch into the sand, to lighten Cassie's mood with a jackpot, but the children's noisy reunion does the job. Harry wheedles a go of the metal detector, which Cassie straps to his thin arm. He takes off. 'That fast, he'll never find anything,' Cassie observes, and once a sentence has slipped through the bars, Janet dares to speak another.

'Cass, I'm sorry. I shouldn't have said those things.'

Cassie holds her ground, not about to shake her resentment. 'When I was little, I used to be jealous of kids who had cancer. Because everyone cared about them. They had telethons and stuffed toys, because people felt sorry for them. People understand that kind of sick. I know what it's like for Harry. He's like me. Not all like me. Just this much.' She measures a sliver of air between her thumb and forefinger, a hair's breadth of belonging.

Janet puts an arm around her sister's hunched shoulders. 'I've got a bit of it, too, Cass. Not a lot. But enough to know. It's part of who we are.' She feels Cassie soften.

'Like our birthmarks,' Cassie says.

Tea-coloured stains, the size of an almond on each back. Neither could see their own but each had described the mark for the other.

A manic beep from the detector tugs Cassie upright and

she rushes to Harry's side. Three pairs of hands dig wildly, the professional telling the children to stay calm or they'll bury their find even deeper. For all her cool, Cassie squeals as Harry recovers a small copper box. Three heads bob in a tight circle of appraisal as she wipes it clean with a rag pulled from a pocket. Then the rain comes, hard and heavy, drenching them in the time it takes to gather shoes and bags and make a run for the car park. The sudden sprint has everyone laughing, except for Harry. He puts on a brave front for Grace, but Janet can see that fear is lapping his nervous system. Their panting mists the windows until the airconditioning clears a view of the storm.

The rain smacks at the windscreen and a ribbon of lightning dives into the sea. 'I'm scared,' Grace cries. Janet wonders whether her admission will undo Harry, as if his anxiety is an air bubble that will fizz to the surface at the first turn of the lid.

But he takes a deep breath and repeats steady words from his mother's phrasebook. 'The car's the safest place to be in a storm,' he reassures Grace, chewing the neck of his shirt.

'The car's useless if you're stuck on a bridge and the river's rising,' Cassie mutters. She clutches on to Harry like a terrified child. 'I'm so scared. I'm always scared and I don't know what to do. Help me!' she quavers in a baby voice.

Janet tenses, waiting for Harry's eruption, but he smiles. He actually smiles.

'You are not scared. You big liar.'

Cassie sticks her tongue out at him, and Harry laughs.

They drive slowly back to Seymour Court, Harry holding on to Cassie's calm like a comforter. The window wipers sweep back and forth in a lost cause.

Janet turns on the radio to distract the children and Cassie sings along, displaying the same capacity that Harry has for recovering from the doldrums or a rage. She croons as if alone on a spot-lit stage, much to the kids' delight.

'Mum's home,' Grace shrieks as they pull into the driveway of 21, behind a trusty Volkswagen advertising its owner's wanderlust with stickers from outback towns.

Annie is a bird of a woman, not so much bigger than Harry. She welcomes Janet and Harry warmly, rustling up afternoon tea and asking easy questions about their day. Grace attaches herself to her mother's hip and Cassie towers over them both, an octagonal peg lucky to have found a niche where she fits, sort of, in a home where shortcomings thrive.

Janet watches Annie bustle around the kitchen, teasing Grace and swapping jokes with Cassie, at ease with her boarder. Cassie fattens the small family, filling up silences with her clumsy talk and indomitable spirit, proud of her purpose.

Rain has made its way inside and Grace is ordered to get a baking tray to catch the water and the dull drip becomes a ping. Cassie finds another leak and improvises with a battered old frypan.

Out the front, Cassie and Janet hug tightly while Grace and Harry say their own goodbyes.

'About today, I'm sorry,' Cassie offers. 'If anything had happened to those kids . . .'

'Nothing did happen.'

Cassie nods but she still looks unsettled. 'I know you think I won't be a good mother, but I can do this.'

Janet wants to grant Cassie's wish, but she can't. 'Do you know how hard it's going to be, bringing up a baby by yourself?'

Cassie shrugs. 'You managed.'

'But I've got a partner, and money. It makes all the difference, Cass.' She takes Cassie's hand, hating herself for saying this. 'You have to be as sure as you can possibly be that going through with this is the right thing.'

'All I know is that it feels right.' Cassie cups a hand around her belly, protective.

'Promise me one thing,' Janet says, pulling her sister close. 'That you'll stay in touch. Whatever happens.'

'Cross my heart,' Cassie replies.

Maybe the art of living well means worrying less, Janet thinks, as she backs out of the driveway too quickly, almost collecting a tail light on the gate post.

'Please can I have a little sister?' Harry starts up, as if they can simply swing into a 24-hour service station and place an order through the intercom. He loved being with Grace and Cassie, apart from the last bit, which he excises, like greens left on the plate.

Janet switches the radio on midway through news of a 75-year-old woman whose body has been found in a nursing home storeroom – stricken with dementia, the woman had found her way into the windowless room by accident, the door locking shut behind her. She thinks of Dale, who up until now has only had her cats to worry about. They'd spoken briefly before the trip, skirting the irony of their separate wars with disorder.

Little families made of ticky-tacky, yet somehow they survive. Harry's protectiveness of Grace, his need to care of someone smaller – these are strengthening goods. And mothering shatters self-absorption's hypnotic hold. Perhaps this will be the making of Cassie.

That night Janet can't sleep. Some nights are like this, locking her out of dreams, upending her. She checks on Harry, asleep with his mouth open, like an old man napping blissfully under a noonday sun. 'Be careful,' he had counselled Grace. She whispers the words back to him and his limbs twitch under the sheets as if he's resisting surrender; a lick of blue blanket is wrapped tight around his wrist.

In the morning he refuses to brush his hair or eat a proper breakfast – he wants cheesecake, not cereal. He drops the tube of toothpaste in the toilet before Janet gets around to cleaning her teeth. At the reception desk there is a parcel addressed to Harry, and Janet recognises Cassie's large scrawl. He rips off the brown paper to find the copper box he'd discovered on the beach. 'Finders, keepers,' says Cassie, in a note crumpled inside.

'What could I keep in here?' Harry asks. 'It's so small.'

Conscious of the jobs that must be done before they leave, Janet is about to dismiss him with, 'You'll think of something.' But instead she stops and sits down beside him and together they shrink the world to its elements. 'Grains of red desert sand,' she suggests. 'Gold dust. A droplet of water.'

Harry joins in the game. 'A lock of hair?'

'You could keep your fear in there,' she says.

'It wouldn't fit,' he says earnestly, and as she laughs, he smiles, seeing the funny side of his quirk.

'Well, why not leave it empty for now and see what turns up?' she offers.

Nodding, he tucks the box in his backpack to show his dad.

Janet apologises to Felix for running late when she finally gets to the studio, but he's so busy chatting to the camera crew, he hasn't noticed. The interview goes better than expected after yesterday's debacle. She guesses that once it's skilfully cut with footage of the lightning man's sound and light shows, the story might arrest even Harvey's peripatetic attention.

They return the hire car, with time to waste in the giftshop choosing presents for Nick and Mel – a book for her and a T-shirt for Nick emblazoned with 'does my gut look big in this?'. Searching in her bag for their boarding passes, Janet hears the rattle of Harry's medication in a bottle stuffed into a side pocket. He hasn't taken a tablet for days. She hurls them into a bin, just as she once used to fling her cigarettes away. No more of these, she decides. Too bad for Miss Dobbin. She'll tell Nick they're done with masking games.

The homecoming has its hiccups. Sydney feels hotter than the country's top end and the closeness unsettles them. The harbour tunnel is gridlocked and this place Harry never likes to be is scarier for the heat rising with the fumes and frustration. In his rush to greet the cat as they spill into the front yard, she claws his arm, drawing blood. Outraged, he flings her off the verandah; she lands on her feet and flees under the house.

Night relieves the city barely, the sun gone but not forgotten as the house shifts and the roof creaks from its passing. For the first time in months Janet welcomes Nick's advances in bed, holding him inside her, getting pleasure by giving pleasure, opening herself to whatever lovemaking brings. She wakes early to the kookaburras outside their window. Nick is already out on his morning run. The sound of Harry's ball belting up

The Unexpected Elements of Love

and down the hall, up and down, up and down, up and down, like the birds' lusty cackle, calls her to greet a morning already rebelling against yesterday's predictions of a change.

AT THE CLOSE of a day visiting nursing homes and dementia units, Dale sees gnarled furniture and overgrown minds everywhere she looks.

'Plenty of inspiration for your father,' Beth says sourly, surveying a room of slumped bodies, jiggling legs and blank expressions. 'Nature at its most interesting and grotesque.'

They are being shown around this aged care lodge by Margaret, a towering woman in vinyl slip-on shoes and beige pants who calls herself the Don. 'D.O.N. As in Director of Nursing'.

'Are you looking for a home for your mother?' the Don asks Dale.

'Not on your life,' Beth barks back.

Margaret is puzzled. 'We just want to make a shortlist of places for future reference,' Dale says with a thin smile, even as she's planning a diplomatic getaway.

Next on the list is Houghton Manor. 'Feast or famine,'

Beth sighs, as they park outside an elegant building boasting a manicured garden of camellias and azaleas bordered by a thick hedge of lavender. The Manor is run on Eden principles, Dale tells Beth. Animals, plants, art and children are welcomed for the diversion they bring.

Kelvin is the manager here and greets them with such warmth that Dale feels sure she must know him from somewhere. Children's paintings hang along the corridor. Peering at the signature in a corner of one work, Dale deciphers the shaky hand of 'Mrs W'. An obese tortoiseshell cat stands its ground in the doorway, refusing to budge for Beth's frame.

Kelvin explains that the art is the work of dementia sufferers. Mrs W's splodges of purple and pink are the memory of hydrangeas from the garden where she had played as a child. Neither Beth nor Dale explain that Roy is an artist, although Beth takes to wondering how her children can conceive of Roy without his shed, his studio – there is no such place anywhere they have been. Winded by all she encounters, she seals herself off hermetically from their research.

Still, she co-operates, comforted by her secret, a single pearl embedded in her being. It sustains her through the round of interviews and consultations that fill their days – Dale is thorough to the point of obsession.

Billy has briefed her on staff–patient ratios, ideal bed occupancy rates and accreditation standards. They are investigating council home- and community-care programs. They have visited a memory clinic. They have spoken to an aged care assessment team.

Roy could live another ten years, wearing a tread in the carpet around the dementia wing. He could spend his afternoons watching television repeats, trapped in the land of ga-ga. Beth knows that she can't repel the imposter inhabiting his body or the plaque cannibalising his brain. Intellectual incontinence musn't claim him, not if she can help it.

DALE FEELS TRAPPED and shivery, as if she's in a dank, slimy hell. Everything's on hold, except her fertility. There's nothing temporary about her shifting home; her choices grow leaner the longer she stays, and she must.

The one thing that's lifted her mood is the SMS that flashed up on her mobile from Warren, the researcher who hadn't shown up at Janet and Nick's on the night of the storm. Now the meddlesome weather is ganging up on them again, throwing down hail as Dale packs a picnic basket for their date at Opera Under the Stars.

'Take a helmet with you,' Beth instructs her, with a teasing grin.

'Well, at least we'll have ice on tap.' Dale rattles through kitchen drawers. 'Have we got any matches, Mum?'

'Candles won't last a minute in this wind, darling.'

'I'm not taking candles. My companion is bringing a gas burner so we can brew coffee.'

Beth is impressed. 'And does he have grape crushers to make wine?'

Dale grimaces. 'He doesn't drink.' They exchange a pout of disappointment. 'I've left lentil soup for you and Dad. There's fresh bread and cheese on the bench. All you have to do is heat the soup and pour.' She kisses Beth on both cheeks. 'I'll fetch Dad in,' she promises. Basket in hand, she steps through the gathering dark in the back yard and knocks on the studio door. The light is on but her father doesn't answer. She knocks again, sharper this time, and calls out to him.

'Coming,' he croaks, opening the door with a burning cigarette stuck between the fingers of his right hand.

'Dad, didn't you give up smoking the night I was born?'

'Did I?' he muses. 'Not that it matters any more.' He draws an arabesque in the air, enchanted by the trail of smoke that chalks the blackboard sky. 'Look after your mother,' he tells her.

'She needs you to heat up dinner. Don't forget.' Dale looks at him curiously. 'Where are you off to, anyway?'

'I have absolutely no idea.' He shrugs. 'But you'll find out. You're the clever one.'

She resists the urge to take him in hand; she's impatient to flee.

'It'll look beautiful from a distance,' he says. 'Close up, though, that's another thing.' He reaches out to draw her into the studio. 'Come and see what your old man's been up to.'

There's a twinkle of quartz in his remarks. This is the first time in years that he's invited her inside the studio but she can't linger. 'Sorry, Dad, I've got to run. But I'll drop by for a visit tomorrow.'

'Tomorrow it is, poppet.' He hasn't called her that since she was a girl.

She drops a kiss on his forehead. Glancing back, she sees him waving, the glowing ember between his fingers a beacon in the blackness. She has a buoyant, sudden hope that maybe this sculpture will resurrect him.

Inside, Beth is staring at the cryptic crossword on her lap. She caught the bug from Mora. Now she's given up on her walks, she sits for hours, expending her energy on this chequerboard of space, pounding her brain as she cracks anagrams and riddles to fill the blanks across and down. The television hums away in its corner. It occupies more of her life since Roy vanished into the studio and the streets, since the silences induced by his fear of speaking out of turn, out of order, out of mind.

The credits for a drama fade into a documentary about Antarctica – an interview with a ship's captain perplexed by the disappearing ice. She thinks of Roy's oar, the life jacket he wore home one day, and it suddenly occurs to her that his sculpture really is alive. That he's building a boat. She can't wait to surprise him with her brilliant deduction. Closing her eyes, she meditates on the television pictures of icy crags that have lost their sharp definition. She imagines polar bears stranded on islands that are shrinking into the sea during the northern summer. The ice is crunchy and soft and loose. She picks up a handful of crystals and the coldness crumbles through her fingers. The glacial shelf cannot bear her weight and she sinks into water that is deliciously clean and freezing. She swims for a larger peninsula of whiteness but she can't secure a grip, however hard she tries. Every time she reaches for the ice, it melts in her hands. The surface is thinner than sand biscuits breaking from the shore's crust after a day of baking sun.

She is frantic and sweating now, hot and tired from treading water. She hears the splinter of glass and jerks awake, startled by the patterns of light dancing on the walls, thrown from somewhere outside.

The studio is on fire. Burning debris scatters through the yard, bags of rubbish airborne, sparks flying. She screams out to Roy but the wind swallows her warble. The house is alight now, the kitchen fire alarm beeping shrilly, its cry lost in the gluttonous rush of the flames. She has a choice. She reaches for Cuz but cannot see for the smoke. Bewildered, she sinks back into the chair and bites her lip, tasting the blood.

THE FIRE'S ASHES were blown into the sea, washing up against the reserve where Roy's sculpture outlives him.

Dale and Billy hadn't wanted Beth's farewell to be overshadowed by the hoopla of Roy's fame. They held a small memorial service for their parents on Observatory Hill, an amethyst of grass tucked beneath the harbour bridge.

Dale remembered the cigarette burning in Roy's hand and cursed herself for the fire. She should have stopped to see her father's work, to keep him company. Billy calls their death a deliverance from much worse; he's heartened that one parent did not survive the other.

Both children attend the unveiling of his sculpture at the meteorological bureau. Janet drives Dale down to Canberra, Harry wriggling all the way, grumpy at being dragged along and unsettled by grey skies that ridicule the forecast of a fine day. As if the weather cares a hoot for predictions.

At the bureau they make their way through the crowd of

public servants, gallery curators, artists and the media. Billy and Dale stop to hug Mora, who calms their nerves even as she nurses her grief, reminding them that this isn't the first time Roy's wagged an opening. Dale is warmed by a joke that her mother could have made.

Phillip Bennett shows them to their seats, front row. Janet sits between brother and sister, wan with the nausea that has been plaguing her for days, but surer now of its source. Harry has free rein, like she'd promised him. He runs off to sniff at the heels of the crowd.

The drone of conversation lulls as Bennett rises to address the audience. As he describes his first meeting with Roy all those years ago, the wind flutters through the forecourt like a late arrival, tugging at the black shroud draped over the sculpture.

Dale imagines her mother's eye on the audience. She would have approved of Mora's maroon cloak and she would have set her daughter straight as to the identity of the sad woman who clutches the brim of her hat as another, stronger gust of wind snaps the cloth from its anchor and the blinding colour of Roy's 'Hot Water' is revealed prematurely, its brilliance undulled by the overcast sky.

At the first suggestion of rain, the guests are ushered inside to eat finger food and talk. Harry pleads to stay outside, for once untroubled by the elements. He whoops around the empty forecourt until he tires of his tricks, then plumps down beside the boat. The wind sends a pile of programs flapping and as the pages scud past, he grabs one. Inside, there is a black and white photograph of the man who made the boat and the story of his life. Harry stares at the picture. It's the man in the life jacket. The man who saved the little girl in the straw hat.

He looks again at the glass boat, interested now. He knows he shouldn't but he scoots under the rope barrier and clambers aboard. The boat is solid and smooth. He loves the candy colours, the crazy tilt of the hull in its glass puddle. He tries to pull the oar, but it's stuck.

Something catches his eye. Carved into the wood is the smallest heart, with the initials B.W. barely decipherable. Even tinier letters beneath this declaration could be mistaken for scratches.

Harry studies the nicks and sees shapes that no one would notice unless they bothered to crawl up close or took the time to search. He concentrates harder, convinced that the shipwrecked man is speaking to him. As the meaning of the words becomes clear he laughs, then sings Roy's dedication to the world out loud. 'Row hard against the tide.'

ACKNOWLEDGMENTS

Thank you to the characters of Beth and Roy for their noisy prompting, which led me to my agent, Mary Cunnane. Her belief in this novel from the very beginning nurtured its growth. Thank you to Kirsten Abbott at Penguin, who imagined a book as she leafed through the manuscript and set to publishing it. I am indebted to my editor, Sandy Webster, for her inspired suggestions, and to my dear friend Simon Hughes, for his counsel.

Thanks to Bettina Arndt, Amanda Buckley, Claire Gerson, Mary Louise O'Callaghan and Christine Wallace for pertinent advice during perilous moments. To my father, John, my mother, Alison, who encouraged me to write, my mother-in-law, Molly, and the heart-lifters amongst my friends and extended family.

Finally, thank you to my husband, Gregory Hywood, for his unstinting love, and to our boys, Jack and Tom, for blessing us with the unexpected elements of life, the bumpy bits and the glorious discoveries that bind us together.